PLAY, A NOVEL

ALSO BY ALAN SINGER

The Inquisitor's Tongue (FC2, 2012)
Dirtmouth (FC2, 2004)
Memory Wax (FC2/Black Ice Books, 1996)
The Charnel Imp (Fiction Collective, 1988)
The Ox-Breadth (New Earth Books, 1978)

PLAY, A NOVEL

ALAN SINGER

grand IOTA

Published by
grand**IOTA**

2 Shoreline, St Margaret's Rd, St Leonards TN37 6FB
&
37 Downsway, North Woodingdean, Brighton BN2 6BD

www.grandiota.co.uk

Cover image: Edward Hopper, *The Sheridan Theater* © 2020 Heirs of
Josephine N Hopper / Licensed by Artists Rights Society (ARS), NY

Acknowledgment: A portion of this work appeared under the title
"Violent Act (Rehearsal)" in *Golden Handcuffs Review*

Typesetting & book design by Reality Street

A catalogue record for this book is available from the British Library

ISBN: 978-1-874400-77-6

To act is to do and to pretend.

What are we doing that is not pretending
when we know that we are acting?

Nicholas Mosley
Catastrophe Practice

Again, for Nora

THERE WILL BE NO INTERMISSION

All stage directions are broadcast through the auditorium over the PA system. The sound is distressed to evoke a bullhorn roaring over the engine noise of a lumbering truck offstage.

Scene 1: A clearing in a fir forest, springing up behind the actors on steel catapults that turn into rigid supports for the prickly green-needled canopy.

Enter Stage Right: Icon is attired as an aristocrat arriving at a cotillion, black waistcoat trailing excessively long tails, with a top hat in his right hand and the dueling pistol swaggering in his left.

The manservant Gibbon is already onstage.

ICON: Blood in the grass.

GIBBON *(gesturing toward a path through the wood with a fox tail nailed to a stick):* This way, sir.

ICON: Yours, I'm afraid.

Icon raises the pistol and shoots.

The actor must be true to the man.

I follow that rule myself. My surgeon is a friend. He has tickled my ventricles. We are to meet for dinner. We are friends who meet. As usual, I am going to play my part: the patient patient. He says he has an *interesting* surgery to recount from this very morning.

Dr Todorow is amused to think of my playing. He confesses for me that I can't help myself. A player from birth, congenital, incapable of acting without acting the part.

He does not know how wrong he is.

Neither is he above the seductions of the stage. He took me as a patient, I have no doubt, for the celebrity of my productions, for the notoriety of my performances. And especially for the mantle of *experimenter* that I don as imperiously as the doctor in his surgery dons the white coat. And now he has taken our friendship as a license to come to the theater when we are rehearsing, to whisper to the playwright who directs his own plays and who has been known to act in them anonymously, as if he, the medical man, could influence the action. He wishes to be seen influencing the scene.

So, who is playing to the better audience?

We will dine on the other side of a wall that is shared by the theater with a bustling trattoria, *La Bussa*. The doctor will indulge his weakness for marrow, *Osso Buco*. I will take the bone itself, the veal chop dressed with barely a teardrop of olive oil and embittered with a sprig of rosemary.

When Furio, our favorite waiter, owl-eyed behind his olive-green spectacles, affecting shoulder-length hair parted in the middle, however thin and greying, flourishes his red-jacketed order pad above his head and turns briskly away from the table, I can see the eagerness glistening on Dr Todorow's lips. He is impatient to recount today's surgery, scene by scene.

"A five-chambered heart! Like a bee!"

How could I resist his enthusiasm for such a conceit?

He paused for me to show interest, to lean closer, until I was inhaling the allergenic scent of the oleander blossom drowned in the oversized table vase between us, no less bloated than the fetus in the bell jar.

"An infant heart, you understand. You appreciate the elements. And what waits in the wings? Let me block it out for you.

"When I am called to the OR, I am already plotting. In the breast pocket of my surgical smock a glass pipette, delicate as the most hairlike artery adorning the palpated muscle of the heart, stands erect. It is clasped in the taut seam of the vermillion pocket stamped with the hospital insignia. I have already inhaled the albino arachnid, no bigger than a crust from the corner of your eye, into the pipette's humidifying constriction. It waits.

"I stand close to the surgical table. I will not lean too far forward over the incision that yawns under the pressure of my index finger. I have my mark, as you might say. I'm standing on it. The paper sheath in which the sole of my shoe is sterilized would erase the markings on the floorboards of your stage. We would undo the performance by rehearsing it.

"My theater is different. We do not rehearse. The hand is the hand. The dome lamp shines as unquestionably as the sun on the scenery. Dr Todorow, if I can be so immodest as to speak of myself in the third person, is a ray of light to his patients. He incandesces amidst the ceremonious and deferential bustling of his impeccably bleached team. In their white scrubs they flank him like the riffling feathers of wings that might be summoned to beat the air in a miracle of ascent.

"The lights, the costumes, the livid momentousness of the infant heartbeat, like a protagonist coming on stage for the first time. The bated breath. All are poised for the action.

"I take my cue. It is all buzzing in my head, all that is to be done, as I press the gleaming flange of the tiny scalpel between my finger pads. I carry the sting of the bee in my hand. Everyone chuckles to hear me call our patient, less than a week old, the *bee girl*. And, truth be told, she has no proper name yet, according to the nurse whose forehead furrows above her vellum mask.

"*Bee girl.* I lower my surgical microscope to the bridge of my nose. I pretend not to be amused by my minute witticism, though I am still looking up. Perhaps I am studying the diagrammatics of the problem. Once the heart is opened, the right atrium, anomalously bisected into two chambers by an interseptum, must be made unitary, whole. The membrane between the chambers may be tough as gristle or airy as a breath of gossamer. I make much of the scale of things. I make a show of finding my focus. I swivel the rings of my scope back and forth, calling attention to the ratcheting. I lean in. I am burrowing into the depth of field. The chambers of the infant heart are minute enough to excuse my probing posture. I wish to give the appearance of a man descending into a hole that is not big enough to accommodate the pupil of the spying eye.

"I relish the eyes upon me like something salubrious in the mouth.

"Have we ordered?"

"Well, you can imagine, dear Pan, that as I commence the most delicate step of the operation my thoughts are awash with some kind of salivary foam. I think especially of the fretful parents tensed before the screen of the monitor that I have set up for them in a remote soundproof chamber, an enveloping white space in which the nervously dilating pupils of their eyes are flailing helplessly. When the latex tips of my fingers are as wet as their eyes, the operation is approaching its *dénouement*. I can see the parents' expectant faces, by reciprocating circuit, on the small television screen reflected in the mirror that is hinged to my headpiece. The screen flickers behind me where no one else would think to look. The parents are holding hands.

"Like lovers at the theater, it occurs to me.

"Well, as you know, good Pan, the action must complicate."

I see that Todorow sees my lashes flutter for him.

"Focus on my hand now. For I am laying down the scalpel. I am feigning a brusque adjustment of the microscope. I am reaching for the pipette in my breast pocket where my own heart is hovering. I will need to bow deeply enough to the table that my swiftest reach for it, the pipette, will be indistinguishable from the expert technician's obligatory inspection of the excavated organ, perhaps the size of a chicken liver. My eye is now where my hand will be in only a few minutes, when the thread of the first suture will plant its kiss upon the puckering tissue. It is, of course, not my eye. The protuberant lens of the eyepiece blinds even my closest collaborators to the furtive maneuver of my right hand, even more furtive by virtue of my ambidexterity. Everyone assumes I am left-handed. So, they are all looking at the point of the needle I lift high above the table in sparkling preparation for closing all the wounds.

"And with my unpredictable, inexplicable right hand, from the pocket that is luffing mere centimeters from the patient's torn breast, I move the pipette to my waiting lips, everything on the same plane now, bent as I am in my official act of concentration. Who would imagine?

"A single, soundless puff dislodges the speck of the spider, like a bead of pollen in a humid breeze.

"Only now, with the privilege of the microscope, can one see the albino spider scintillate against the livid gleam of the ventricular wall. Clutching. Tarsus and claw.

"A life hanging in the balance. On a thread, you might say, if you were a spider lover.

"Letting my hand drift audibly against the folds of my surgical apron, I cover the sound of the pipette snapping between two knuckles. I let it drop to the brittle floor of the OR with the accompaniment of a camouflaging grunt. There the ball of my foot renders it dust."

The arrival of the plates – at first the waiter misplaces the dishes, requiring a circuit around the table that causes Todorow to break the spell of his narrative with a violent twisting of his neck – gives me a moment to digest, so to speak, the substance of the plot as it has been developed. But I am hungry, too. The fatty whiff of singed bone draws me to my own place at the table. The knife in my hand will be in no way as momentous as Dr Todorow's. But it will sever the tale from his lips.

Which is just as well. For the moment, it should suffice that we fill our mouths with meat. And as I might say to Todorow, though I don't dare, every play can benefit from an intermission. If nothing else, the break reminds the audience of their own time. It gives them pause. Time is time to think.

And what would they think of? That all that Todorow had meant to happen happened for show. That a licensed medical procedure in a well-regarded public hospital of our metropolis was co-opted to the private urges of a melodramatic temperament. There's no doubt of that. It would not have been unfair for me to say that "if you think life and death are more real in your play than in mine, let me remind you that you have never killed anyone." Unless you consider the spider. Would a speck of spider survive the closing of the wound, after all?

But I cannot ask the question without ruining the effect. The effect. It is what we both strive for. Even the audience is a prop of the play. I would no sooner let myself obtrude a fictitious skepticism about the unfolding of my dear friend's drama-in-mind than I would permit the collapse of a wall onstage to interfere with my plans to play things out to the end. I would not deny him his effect.

I let my mastication of the bloody chop speak for itself. As though he knew I were being charitable with him in the private perch of my critic's box, Todorow took up the slack of his playlet with a pricking word.

"Pierced. I had pierced the enchambering wall of an anomalous infant heart, you know. First, I had pierced it to determine its resistance to the keen edge of the scalpel. And when I had determined the membrane's vulnerability, when I understood what degree of focus it would give the blade by its resistance, I had sharpened that focus further against the whetstone of my eye and excised the membrane altogether. That was the success of the procedure. The spider, snugly sutured within the new chamber, was the itch of suspensefulness for me, of course."

His magician's gaze, scouring my face for any vestige of incredulity, assured me that his suspensefulness had a false bottom.

"I take it though, by the smoothness of your brow and by the salubrious ease of your chewing, my distracted Pan, that you have no fear of a mere dot of a spider, barely the spittle of my breath.

"But you forget the possibility of venom."

I had indeed imagined the curtain coming down upon my mind's-eye view of the applauding faces crowding the gurney and showering such light on the spectacle of the closing wound.

"Not so fast," he didn't say. But I knew this was the predicament Todorow had set for me. I had rushed myself. Such was the puzzlement he no doubt imagined he could wriggle onto the smooth brows of all those who didn't even know there was a spider. Then how could they have known that a moment existed between the spider's ability to strike and its suffocation in the living tissue, suturing the life of the patient to a healthy future? I would have to think about that.

They would not have imagined it, unless it happened.

The question would so belatedly be, "How could it have happened?"

Then Todorow made note of the members of his audience, not least of all the relieved, for the moment, parents. They were held unwittingly captive in the cramped screen of the video monitor that was in fact Todorow's mind's-eye incarnate, nestled, as he had already confided to me it was, in the background of the action. Then there was the bright-eyed and smeary-mouthed anesthesiologist, already coiling his tubes into their snake-charmer baskets. The three nurses, clenching hands upon the rails of the gurney, are responsible for what happens now, now the worst dangers are past, or so they think. Confidence shines in their faces as gleamingly as the steel in their grip as they prepare the pilgrimage to the recovery room. Only the beeping, red-eyed heart monitor remains to be harnessed for the journey.

It was the monitor that caught them off guard. Suddenly shrilling. Without warning, the sound of emergency clamored urgently about them. Todorow could see them summoning the muscles in their faces to meet the alarm, as purposefully and as palpably as the hands they relaid upon the instruments they had only just relinquished.

He confided that he relished the likeness to naked

bathers scrambling to clothe themselves against the gaze of an unwelcome public breaking raucously into the secluded bower of a lazy riverbank where, having dropped the facade of dress, the innocents are dripping. One has seen it in paintings.

So, I might have known. Todorow had contrived it himself. He had tampered with the equipment in time to seize the moment for his most suspenseful purposes. They had all imagined they knew what was coming next.

Now something *was* coming, bearing down without direction, but with dire proximity. The startle reflex was enough to freeze the characters in gestures of ignorant intent. The parents, rushing to exit the white door in the white cubicle, saw the fingers of their hands spread out before them, wriggling blindly for a grip on the moment. The tottering stature of the anesthesiologist, he having already pricked his finger on the syringe of epinephrine, was thrown back against the wall of the OR in the pose of the snake charmer bitten by his familiar. The three nurses found each other's hands in the instrument bay where they had reached for handles, knowing blades lurked dangerously in their places.

Plain to see. A tableau. A scene of panic. But Todorow was peering at *me* through the marrow-less aperture of his last shin bone, his lips heedless of the orange drippings puddling his plate.

He obviously knew the fates of the others. Only I could wonder the fate or the fatality of the spider. I was the interesting one now. The one to watch. The one whose eyes would tell the success of the lurking surprise. Or so I thought he thought.

Wrong again.

Pre-empting any doubt as to his success, Todorow abruptly spoke. Pushed into the footlights by his stalwart company of players now the curtain was down, his smile was as sinuous as the author's most artful bow.

Nor was the author waiting for applause. Surely he noticed me sitting back in my chair, wiping a napkin haplessly over the wine blotches I had dribbled down my shirt front.

Already too delighted with himself, he divulged the secret in the most hastily self-congratulatory tone of voice: "And of course it was the test button on the heart monitor that so falsely alarmed the room. The pressure of my knee under the table. I mean the gurney.

"I call it *The Fall of the Wall of Atrium.*"

Scene 6: A lofty turret room of the renegade Gonzogo's castle. Stone walls streaked with a furry dampness. Instruments of torture: a rack, pulleys, hooks.

Gonzogo is cinching Rosalinda's wrists to the rack. She barely resists.

GONZOGO: Look upon these remnants of previous leather bindings. Are they not curled against the dowels like perched birds mortally fastened to bare lime twigs?

ROSALINDA: My limbs will not survive the test. Why not cut out my tongue to soothe your wrath, since it will warble the notes of my innocence forever in your hearing?

GONZOGO: That tongue I should have cuddled with my lips? It would have been my pleasure to make it my pet, were it not such a cur to the truth.

ROSALINDA: Signore, my only falsity was the truth of my love for Fernando, whose bones your axe set to as if you were a chopper of wood. So, you watered the tree of your hatred with his blood. We did see how it rose to the knees of your breeches, you waded so deep.

GONZOGO: I will go deeper yet.

ROSALINDA: In me, with your roughest blade. Be quick!

Gonzogo reaches for the dagger in his belt.

ROSALINDA: But stay. Do you not wish to know what it would have been like had I parted my lips for you? Thusly, at least you might know what you have slain.

GONZOGO: What? Give me reason to do honorably that which would otherwise have seemed dishonor? Defile a slut? By your leave mistress, I will.

By the scruff of her neck, Gonzogo wrenches Rosalinda's mouth toward his own. When he crushes his mouth against hers, Gonzogo gives an agonized shriek and falls backwards to the floor. Rosalinda cries out. She bares her incarnadine teeth. The bloody tip of a sewing needle glints minutely in their grip. She spits.

ROSALINDA: Quicker am I to the scabbard of my tongue than you to the scabbard on your belt, Signore. To be plain, the point of my blade was already tipped with the adder's bile. The bite at the other end of the needle was easy enough for me to bear, knowing how my taunting tongue, skewered on the very shaft of the needle, would bid you good death.

Marry, my tongue bleeds from the wound that wombed the needle's sting. I would not deny it. Unlike yourself, I do bleed the evidence of a murder.

But you, Signore, you are dead.

"Yes. The piece has a working title: *Killer Killing Killers*. Many scenes, but all superficially disarticulated from one another. Except of course that they are all scenes of murder. One after another. Murder keeps them interested."

How many times have I begun the conversation with my potential backers this way?

As with my surgeon, we meet in restaurants. Or in the bars that are anterooms to restaurants. Pretexts for eating. For acting. It is an act of devotion, if I can conjure it from their hip pockets.

My potential backers wish to divine the meaning of their investment. It is my job to make them believers, in the very manner of the original mystery players. The devil could bare his backside onstage and no one would laugh at the shagginess of the hair that whipped the swagger of that dark orifice. Well, I want them to take it on faith that their money is already a token of sacred knowledge, which no accountant could ever divulge for them. They require instead the offices of a priest of dramaturgy.

Is it not art, after all, that we are discussing, glasses in hand, our mouths quite full?

"Think of *yourself* as the meaning of the play," I tell them. "Do you not recognize your special sensitivity to the human condition?" Then I delve into the body cavity, stroking the choicest organs. The stomach, the heart. I conjure a plot, a fate. I make a character stoop. I unfold a fabric of suffering, spread it out before them.

"The production is a sort of tablecloth upon which we will break bread. Such knowledge of the human heart we will purvey." I inspire them to appreciate our partnership. "You in your capacity as a producer, me in my capacity as a producer of miracles."

So I inveigle them, knowing how insatiable the hunger for the right feeling can be. Touching human organs is a tricky business. Not to say 'sticky'. You want to breathe life into the idea of the play. You want them to feel the fragility, the shortness of that breath. And you want them to stomach it when you suck that breath away. But be chary of the heartstring too tautly strung. Don't snap the bond by suturing things too tightly. Well, I sound like a medical man myself. No surprise there.

Believe me, I have spent my hours on the table dying to be the surgeon, not the rattling patient. Dying, if truth be told.

It can indeed be told.

***

Dr Todorow stirred in his seat, in the fifth row, center of the Crooked Hat Theater, observing my high-stepping entrance from stage left. The stage set, a curved wall of mirrors, reversed that direction for the audience, held briefly as they might have been in the grip of illusion. Not least the illusion that here was a healthy specimen of an actor.

No such illusion would hold sway over the unconfoundable heart-carver. As he tells it, he was already alive with the foreknowledge that hums in the fingertips of a man whose senses press against unpredictable densities of tissue, even as they yield to the blade of whetted steel. Such is the surgeon's preternatural attunement to what is next. We all squirm in our balcony seats with the tickle of such anticipation in our tails. Who can help it? Well, we are not doctors, after all – we cannot help.

As I set my tiptoeing foot to the floor behind Siegfried, the magician's wand-waving figure, the garrote dangling from my fingertips like a shimmering necklace, my entire physique shuddered with the first fist-thumping blows of the heart muscle within my breast. The even more massive thump of my entire body upon the floorboards of the stage, as tremorous as a sandbag plunging from the lighting grid above our heads, caused Siegfried the magician, meant as he was to be caught unawares by the garrote that was skittering across the stage, to flinch and cower. Precisely the response that my character's exaggerated lightfootedness was intended to forestall. The director should have halted the production.

But an unsubtle foot was now stomping its way from my chest to my shoulder and down my arm, finding its mark, so that the obligatory recognition scene of my personal Aristotelian tragedy, all too horribly recognizable to me now, might unfold to its fatal conclusion.

Luckily, luckily I had a secret collaborator in this drama that I could not have authored by myself. Dr Todorow's rush to the stage outpaced the giant foot treading upon the life that I now imagined to be a mouse scurrying frantically to escape the enclosure of my narrowing chest. He found me athwart the mark where the stage action was meant to have progressed, my eyes spread wide and overflowing with light from the pole grid above our heads, my arms and legs flung awry, the body trying to save itself by reckless abandonment of the convulsing torso.

He knew what to do. He seized the mouse tail. With my pulse still throbbing under his thumb, he raised himself on one knee beneath the wash of a glaring spotlight that must have made the squinting spectators wonder if this wasn't a continuation of the drama in which they were so engrossed. Passing his open hand across the face of the audience, as if to wipe the greasy film from a window, he ordered the auditorium to be cleared.

The ambulance might have disgorged from his mouth, it appeared with such instantaneity. Its siren, hovering over my lurching stretcher as we raced out of the bleak tunnel of my breast-beating terror into the salvific illumination of the operating theater, still rings in my ears. Someone was holding my hand, leading me on. Voices spoke as though I were their echo chamber. They did not speak to me. I was scissored free of my clothes and shifted from gurney to table. A heavy glove was placed upon my mouth. I breathed it in as I was instructed. I felt vague fingers snuggling in my nostrils, in my throat.

As the fur grew thicker in my consciousness, I was nonetheless aware that another stage awaited my appearance. Dr Todorow's eyes beamed the key light that I chillingly recalled only the risen dead can give report of. My complete loss of consciousness at that moment did not dim the scene of action that was about to transpire, though I was no audience for it. They trotted out my heart. It took its bow.

I'm making an inference. I am, after all, alive.

***

An inference, fittingly enough, is what I ask of my potential backers. I don't deny it. For them it might be characterized as the leap of faith that one hopes will be fortuitously winged with success. I am the one, am I not, promising to make those wings sprout?

I felt the nibs of those wings scratching my throat while we waited for the first drinks to arrive. The bardic genius who first dipped his quill into the inkpot was at the feathered end of the bargain. So, I must flock to answer their questions. I am, after all, one of a company.

"Yes, the piece has a working title. *Killer Killing Killers*. You can take it either way. Either the killer is adjectivally motivated, a killing kind of killer. Or have it otherwise: the killer kills. Of course, if you try to go one way, the other will follow."

My potential backers are of the world that knows the difference between an adjective and a noun. They aren't cunts, as our Pinter would have a character say. I have taken part in his audiences at the more fashionable theatrical houses, no doubt among the likes of the backers sitting before me now. They sport turtleneck sweaters, cashmere scarves, ascots – not cowboy hats and string ties. They speak languages that did not mother them. They have traveled extensively. They have gorged on exotic meats in exotic locations. They have attained their full stature as men and the occasional startlingly attractive woman. Their photographs, among the faces of other directors, playwrights and actors, stare out at us from the walls of even such restaurants as this, where I invite my potential backers to swirl the wine in the glass, to lean back against padded leather and entertain my proposal. Yes, the drinks had arrived.

"But don't get the wrong idea. There is humor. The humor, you see, is in the blood. Think of the old humors of the blood that would have bubbled in the bard's time and you're approaching the insight that is my tickling inspiration. I seem to give you only violence in my play – seemingly discrete scenes, like blood-soaked bread-crumbs dropped without a pathway to remember. But my audience will pick them up. They will see the humor of it in the end, because they have no choice.

"I've been accused by my critics of worse convolutions, believe me.

"So, yes, the play is one scene after another of killing. But one thing after another implies a history, does it not? The meaning will, of course, be recognizable to my audience by cues of costuming and scenery, if not by the distinct idioms echoing our hoary theatrical past. Each scene will be dressed out in the costuming and language of our Greeks, our Elizabethans, our Jacobeans, our Victorians, our contentedly absurd Moderns, the whole playlist of our great masters. The dignity of the theater itself is to be honored in these scenes, despite the rampant gore.

"So, at least seemingly, it will be one scene after another of the knife piercing the eye, the garrote nearly severing the vertebrae (there are tricks to this trade), the bullet still smouldering in the victim's chest, the poniard twisting in the groin, the anal penetrations with the fire-dripping iron poker (tricks, as I say). But *seemingly* is the point.

"Because you haven't heard the best part yet. You haven't really understood what it is I am proposing. And that's as it should be. Your suspense is the audience's suspense. You will know what they will know, unexpectedly, as it happens in the most realistic way. I am a mimetic artist, you see, quite contrary to the label *experimentalist* which critics have stitched upon the fabric of my career and which, like all the white-coated laboratorists who so dutifully attend to our mortality, simply frightens the audience away. Some call them doctors.

"I tear that label out of the lining of every performance.

"Well, here is the proof of my plot-making proficiency. One scene after another of killing, etc. One scene after another of the knife piercing the eye, etc. Oh, they'll get the gore, our audience. They may even be briefly startled by their capacity for boredom, the edge of their seats numbing the backs of their legs. They'll get the gore. But they'll have missed the point of the poniard, if you catch the flourish of its twinkling in my eye. Until they have seen enough, until they have seen past the costuming, even past the face paint.

"'But he is already dead,' they will now mutter to themselves. One killer killed by the next in scene after scene. Such is the appearance they will have been given by us jointly, should you take my hand in this venture. Now they will feel the confidence of their smug judgment in the smile-primped corners of their lasciviously rouged lips. Men are plumped with as much blood as women in the snide curling of the lip that accompanies the presumption to criticize.

"For the killer has, with each killing, taken a bow of sorts. Releasing his weapon of choice to the incriminating clatter of the stage floor, the killer has turned full face to the aghast audience before abruptly exiting the scene, until the next scene, and the next, when the actor's face will be recollected ever more sharply.

"So now they will be embarrassed for the actor, even more so for the writer and producer whom they will believe have let the theatrical sleight slip from the hand. They will begin to presume.

"'The same actor,' they will whisper to one another. 'They are using the same actor. How are we meant to believe in these characters if we can see right through the disguises?'

"They won't know that they were intended to mouth these criticisms until the actor speaks for herself.

"In the final scene she addresses herself directly to the audience.

"When she turns to peer over her shoulder, they feel the massive liquid queasiness of the passengers in a lifeboat lifted by a sudden swell rolling off the back of a whale. So, the memory comes to each member of the audience. In every one of the preceding scenes the killer has curiously paused, just so. Before taking the first steps towards his hasty escape, he has paused. He has turned his face to the audience in exactly this way, as if he has had something to say. Then, thinking better of it, tucking himself into the folds of silencing darkness that have closed behind him at the back of the stage, he is gone.

"But this time, after so many scenes of carnage, he speaks. She speaks. 'I've been watching you. How did you not notice? I – I am always the killer.'

"What the audience thought they had unmasked as the disqualifying artifice of the performance was, of course, the point of the performance.

"Well, this reversal of roles is what I'm thinking of now. For the ending. Not bad, I admit. But much can change in the course of rehearsals and rewritings, the accidents of time that stretch before us to opening night. The final ending will come later. You must permit your-selves the suspense. What's a plot without a reversal of fate? His? Or hers?

Final Scene (subject to revision)

A butcher's shop. White-tiled walls. A high counter with a broad view of displayed meats.

Before the counter, Smartson is just leaving the stage, stepping over the hacked corpse of his wife, Sofia, his grip unrelenting upon the axe handle. The axe head bobs drippingly over his left shoulder.

SMARTSON: *He stares with a new and frenzied concentration over his right shoulder at the audience. Here commences a monologue.* I've been watching you. How did you not notice? I, I am always the killer.

You've seen me, perhaps. But you haven't noticed.

And if you are keener of eye than I imagine, you knew I was always the killer, in every scene, whatever the scene, whatever costume I colored it with. I was always the purveyor of this eye [*winks at audience*], tossed over my shoulder like a coin to sop you with, to distract you, as I spirited myself from the stage. Always the same ending. At the terminus of each scene you know what to expect, so far ... as far as you know, anyway.

Were you of keener eye, you would not have been fooled by the appearance that I was always killed in the subsequent scene, an actor dressed like me, who spoke like me, my name his again. If you are of keener eye, hungry for notice, you might say, under your breath, mildly, laughingly to your seatmate, *It's the same actor killing again.*

But still, you've missed a thing or two.

You thought that I, a man murderer, was a man.

Turning to face the audience, unbuttoning the all-too-conspicuous fly of her pinstriped trousers, and with the violent affection of a mother plucking her toddler's arm from a roadway full of careening vehicles, she releases a springy rubber phallus from the flapping vent.

Then, emitting the shriek of a woman who has just stepped over a mouse, she rips open the black velour-trimmed tuxedo vest – fastened from first button to last under the suit jacket – watch fob flying, and looses one alabaster bosom from the false shirtfront now crumpled around her neck. The rosy nipple is pertly erect under her provocative fingertips, proving its authenticity, at least to the first three rows.

BLACKOUT

And my own fate? I began the story of my life, saved by Dr Todorow. Might I finish?

I've said it already. All that I remember of the wailing judder that was my ambulance ride to the sainted hospital – it might have been St Jude – was the good doctor's attempt, despite the best efforts of the emergency medics, to preserve the mask of my face paint. It was the face of Siegfried the magician's resentful assistant, the corners of the mouth and eyes primped with devilish black darts. In retrospect, this oddity of Dr Todorow's behavior was perfectly in character with what I now know of him.

But me first.

I was the emergency. I am told that I arrived under the fluorescence of the blood-lettered EMERGENCY ROOM, drifting in and out of consciousness. But I covet a recollection, brimming with consciousness, which I will testify to with as much passion as any Lazarus who has staggered from the grave with cracked but spittling lips. Just as the ambulance doors were flung open and my gurney was launched upon the hectic tide of hospital protocol, as I slid under his gaze, I heard the doctor's words: "You look perfect."

Then the black curtain fell, heavy and deafening. So, I rely upon the reviews!

I am told that my heart stopped cold on the surgical slab. Well, my mind is never far from the grave.

The moment was apparently made even more dramatic by the knowledge that the blood blackened in my veins. Suspense. The patient was hovering between life and death, as they say. Subsequently, I interviewed the staff who were present in the surgical footlights that night, to gather the threads of the story. And others. Spectators. Their feet had sweltered in the narrow-welled tiers of the stadium seating of the surgical theater, where the heat from the hospital boilers vented stiflingly. It was seating that would ordinarily have been reserved for medical students.

But it was midnight.

On a Tuesday.

And the doctor so craves an audience.

Thus was Siri, my most trusted confidant, among the company of fellow actors, all of whom were admitted to that privileged balcony on the basis, I am sure, of their vivid portrayals of anguish and consternation.

Siri's report of the emergency began with a grimace and a chuckle.

"Your chest was already prised open. The gloved hands were dripping. Your face, a sliver of blue cuddled within the folds of white sheeting, appeared to be turning to stone.

"Well, sweetie, we figured you were already shaking hands with the departing soul. One arm was crookedly thrust out from under the covers, free of whatever binding harness was hidden beneath it. And the fingers of that hand were, sure enough, clasped around something, God knows. Blue as hell, too.

"There was Dr Tod looking up as into blue sky. But he was eyeing his audience. His eyes, bugging out on the struts of magnifying lenses, floating free of his face, might have reached us like soap bubbles blown from a child's lips, burbling into the clouds from the steadying ground of a Sunday park excursion. That kind of innocence.

"Then he tilted his gaze into the dark waters of your chest cavity, at what must have been the critical moment.

"His hands dove within.

"Well, my live darling, he produced nothing less than your heart itself. And then, firmly gripping it in one hand, its red and blue wires torqueing and squiggling in recoil against his grip, he gave it a firm slap with his free hand, the way I imagine a neonate's rump is meant to be slapped. It sounded like applause.

"And why not? He'd started you breathing again! We heard the catch of breath over the ominous rhythms of the beeping monitor that had goosed the suspense. The twists and turns of whatever rewiring he did behind the curtain of our comprehension – you now know better than I, from Todorow himself – and from the hectic charts that they're always saying are your own. Good luck finding yourself in the trickiness of that mirror!"

I interjected. "The patient knows nothing. His body shuts the door behind itself, the last visitor before lights out."

"Well, you're alive, aren't you, my darling? Self-evidence is such a comfort.

"So," she continued, "there he was anyway, taking a modest bow – or was he simply returning the curiously egg-shaped organ to its warming thoracic nest? – then looking up, batting his eyelids against the beatific fluorescence of the operating theater, having restored you to the world of the living, the breathing, the coughing, the snoring, the sneezing and all the rest of it. A moment before, you had appeared to have none of those options available to you.

"Well, sure, he could have sold tickets to a show like that. The bring-them-back-from-the-dead show always forms a line. And it couldn't bother you, my egoless Pan, could it, that you are all *you* have to show for it. Or could it?"

***

It did bother me, of course, or I would never have forced the tale, like so much slippery afterbirth, from Siri's ruby lips. After all, no one stops me on the street to exclaim at the aura of rebirth that I am convinced shimmers around me every moment of my postmortem existence.

If I wish to illuminate my stage, I must make do with the lights that spark from a massive circuit board behind the scenes.

Am I ungrateful? I have a better question: Which of us would be content to be the saved if he could be the savior instead?

Which brings me back to Dr Tod, as Siri so facetiously foreshortened him. At six foot ten, elevated somewhat higher by the shiny greying pompadour that he grooms with ampules of animal oils and matching silver brushes, he can afford to be brought down a bit.

We are friends now. But I don't spare him the strain to his neck, having to hold forth against a stature like mine. I'll have him bending at the waist before we finish one of our almost daily debates about the way things should be onstage. We meet as frequently in rehearsal rooms as at *La Bussa*, our mandibles working as conscientiously in argument with one another as they might over a plate of our favorite artichokes. Our post-operative friendship is a contest as much as a meal. Everything is a bone of contention between our gnawing egos. We whittle away, without respite, at the finer points of stagecraft: how small a prop could be deployed, how quiet a whisper, how dim a key light, how distant an onstage figure could stand before he would go unnoticed by the audience. So passionate is our common interest in deceiving the audience.

And who are they, each so-called member of the audience, if not someone to be recreated by the imaginative author or director whose imagination *they*, after all, have summoned themselves to the theater to judge? Is there a more compelling dramatic conflict we should concern ourselves with than that between actor and audience? Not really, you have to admit. But not many of us are honest enough to do so. Todorow is one such.

How odd that he is a medical man and I his medicine.

I don't say this because the beat of my heart is the refrain of a song he seemed to sing in his spotlit halo, standing wide-armed, open-mouthed, upon the operating theater floor on the night he saved my life. Todorow didn't sing it, nor was he its composer.

That ditty is already thumping in everyone's ear when we lay our heads upon the pillow in the darkened sleep chamber. There, alone with the beating of the solitary heart, in the middle of the night, the loneliness seems unstoppable. Of course, we forget that we are all there together – an audience, you might say, if only we could be so comforted – each of us sitting next to one another in the chill blackness of the cosmic auditorium, invisible elbow to invisible elbow. Are we not company for one another in the rhythms of such knowledge?

Scene 8: Dungeon of the Inquisition

Kenton is strapped to an iron table, his head gripped vice-like in a wooden box. The box is torqued by a screw, big enough to be a ship's wheel, that protrudes from under the table.

Enter Mangan, unsteadily bearing a lead beaker that fumes between the pincers of a pair of tongs. He is enveloped in a black caftan, hooded, his face downcast, hence invisible to the audience.

MANGAN: The elixir of immobility! Shall I decant it into the pitcher from which you are still refusing to pour what could be your dousing words?

Kenton spits.

Mangan pours.

And now Kenton's face appears to be suffused with a crimson light reflected from the ribbon of silk that uncoils sinuously from the canted mouth of the beaker. The ribbon of what is meant to appear to be molten lead is snagged by Kenton's jaws. His bite draws the ribbon taut. He is ingesting, stoking his ample cheeks with bundling silk. It should give the appearance of an imminent combustion. The stage effect is clinched by an exhalation of cigarette smoke that the actor has held captive in his throat since the curtain went up for this scene.

With Mangan's head tilted far enough back that the black cowl slips from his bald and shining pate, he slivers his eyes at the audience and, almost imperceptibly, winks.

But what can Todorow mean when he tells me that his wife will not stand for it? I am well attuned to the first whispers of a plot afoot. But I hear only the breath on his tongue emphasizing the knowledge he is sharing with an uncharacteristically damp and muddily doggish insistence.

He says nothing more.

Though I have called him friend these past ten years, the oddities of the man never cease to amaze me.

***

Todorow's wife, Sigrid, bit me when we were first introduced.

I had taken her hand for the mock formality of a kiss. I imagine we each meant to appear amusing enough to one another, that we might be a match for the merriment of her husband's eyes. When Todorow announced the prospect of this introduction at the end of several seasons of dinners we had shared, he anticipated that his wife and I would enjoy each other's company.

"She is another aficionado of your talent."

Before I could fully raise Sigrid's plump white hand to my parting lips, she had planted her lips upon me, baring her teeth, tugging the skin from the back of my hand.

"Charmed." The word choked out of my mouth. The doctor's frau was peering into my aghast mouth like an examining physician rooting for tonsils. Another doctor. She was, in fact, a child psychologist, unquestionably familiar with the ways of biters.

Turning towards my host in the foyer of what appeared

to be an entirely glassed-in penthouse, transparent to all onlookers at the windows of the surrounding residential towers, I quipped:

"Your bride is a vampire." Though I struggled to shape the words into a congenial witticism, I never attained the full smile that was pulling at the corners of my mouth as forcefully as the medical hand cinching the last suture of a puckering wound. *It takes one to marry one,* I might have smugly conjectured, in a state of lesser extremis. I merely sighed.

Todorow said nothing. He beamed at us from face to face – the one belonging to his astounded friend, the other to his lip-smacking beloved – giving the impression of a somewhat frenzied searchlight scanning a desolate horizon.

"You should know, my Sigrid has thespian ambitions of her own."

Sigrid's grey eyes went dead black beneath the silver helmet of her coiffure. Like her husband, she towered above me. This made the shaking of her body from the shoulders down – the head was as immobile as a ladleful of lead cooling in its mold – all the more seismic. Then she fell into my arms, which I had not been aware of holding out for her. Did I mention that she is a large woman, with the heft of a salon-sized Persian carpet rolled to its tightest cylindrical density, the hauling of which would require at least two men?

Much later I learned of her professionally discreditable reputation for uncompassionate care. She chilled the fretful minds and feverish bodies of her small charges in the public pediatric wards of the city. She had been discharged from one hospital after another: "Incapable of empathy." So her reputation grew.

Breathing heavily under her dead weight, I made a concession to the moment. "You would make a terrific femme fatale."

After all, Sigrid was *playing* for me, the heralded off-Broadway director, whom she suspected of possessing the kind of ego that would succumb to her antic display with equally clever improvisation.

From famished wolf to femme fatale. I had to applaud such versatility.

The intuition of the theatrical director is at least equal to that of the medical diagnostician. So I had utter confidence in my judgment that here, in the foyer of her own apartment, before an invited guest, she was auditioning herself.

She rolled her head toward Todorow, but nestled into my shoulder. In two lithe steps she was leaning into my involuntary embrace. My embarrassment was her divan.

"May I treat my new friend to a game, darling?"

The game was, of course, already underway. But now I would, I decided, *play* for her. Play along.

"Who am I?" she teased.

With that question, she freed herself from my tremblingly supportive arms, improvising a better space in which to display the answer – or in which to dangle the clues on a baited hook. At last the plot was in motion. And despite her heft, she proved unexpectedly agile.

She then stepped away from us both, dropped her husband's bony paw, turned as self-consciously as someone stepping into a spotlight, and began to gather the features of her *character* into the expressive clutches of straining facial muscles. Otherwise, she had a plain face: eyes, nose, cheeks, chins – a doughy mass randomly impressed with kneading thumbs.

But now she managed to straighten the line of the nose with a tip-wiggle. By pulling at the corners of her mouth with a sinew that might have been torqued in the astringent focus of her pupils, she brought cheekbones into relief. And then my surprise turned ominous in recognition of the bright orange hue she hastily applied to her lips. It had been to hand all along in some secret pocket of her remarkably polymorphous physique. Her lips now shimmered with a disarming familiarity. But I let her go on.

Sigrid cast a stony eye on her husband. He stepped back, leaving me exposed to her performance. The look she gave Todorow was a bid. The confidence of the well-rehearsed performer emboldened her to make a bid for applause with her entrance into the light. Bidding the audience up before they even know what there is to be wagered. Between husband and wife it is perhaps easier to guess.

She raised her voice an impressive octave:

"It is I!"

She held her husband's stare as if clutching his chin in the grip of her taut fingers.

"It is I!"

Who the "I" was remained to be seen as she turned away from Todorow and let her gaze fall full on me.

Her shoulders slouched. Their weight immediately transferred to the slinky locomotion of her hips. She thrust one leg straight out, so that its limber partner, drawn passively into its wake, joined the dance with effortless suavity. And those hips walked off with her.

My rushed entrance into the apartment had let the door swing open behind me. Was she about to make an exit?

But no. This was no curtain-caller. The good doctor's wife was merely using the space to her advantage. Leave a door open and anything can pass through. The sensitive performer makes the audience alert to this fact.

Sigrid passed me, turned, shut the door with the heel of her hand, which caused her fingers to wriggle provocatively, first one hand then the other. Her head bobbed from side to side with an oriental flourish.

I had followed her orbit on a pivoting foot. I was now moving on a mysterious axis, clutched somewhere within my alert being like the needle of a compass. And now, facing her, I realized that I stood aligned with her husband, both of us staring with the empty eyes of the expectant audience.

Then the wriggling fingers traveled to Sigrid's midriff. This sent waves through her shifting hips. No doubt we, her private audience, were meant to feel a rhythmic shifting of the ground we stood upon.

Because there she was, already reshaping herself, which explained the choice of the adhesive, flesh-colored leotard in which she had chosen to make my acquaintance. She mimed the charmer's snake, entangling herself in motions that, with each twist of a shoulder or hip, each flexing of an elbow or bending back of the wrist, fed the animus of the entanglement. Foot in hand she twisted her right leg over her left shoulder. She torqued her head back and forth to make it fit through the crook of her knee. It was not however until her descent on the bended knee of her sole supporting leg, her chin rising through the tightening noose of its partner and rising in inverse rhythm with the lowering of her hips and torso, that the words "Twisted aren't I?" spelled out my recognition of how perfectly she resembled an ape.

The words spoken by Siri in her brave and convoluted performance as the carnival contortionist in my sorely under-appreciated production of *The Woman Who Untied Herself* made Sigrid finally appear to me as her own most purposeful self. Not just an actor, an actor in her own right! But my critical litmus test – the newspaper hacks should probe so intimately – would be the effect this performance had upon her husband.

She had induced a rush of blood to his face more alarmingly than a fever propels the mercury to the calibrated heights of a thermometer.

The scintillating orange gloss that Sigrid had applied to her succulent lips at the commencement of this brilliant re-enactment was the poisoned kiss of her plot. Dénouement.

Siri's trademark color. Siri's lips.

This must have been the clue Sigrid discovered for herself, tattooed on her husband's shirt-collar when, one afternoon, on the brink of domestic laundering, she came to know the shame and outrage of being employed as a mere housemaid in the cast of her husband's own, now traumatized, drama of philandry.

Siri herself was lighter, slimmer, slighter, a figure of

such delicacy that if she had entered Sigrid's body, like the patronizing muse, she would have been clutched too tightly in the performer's embrace and broken. But for Todorow, the philandering husband, his wife's performance inspired vision enough of his mistress' allure. So he blushingly suffered the pressing thumb of Sigrid's judgmental gaze upon him when she was done.

Finis, indeed.

Did I expect a bow? Was the entertainment concluded? Why did I feel a compunction to swallow the smile that was smeared on my lips?

Because I understood the meaning of the performance, that's why. To arouse a moist intimacy between husband and wife. Tears, not the less astringent juices of coitus. How better to tell the wicked philanderer that one knows of the betrayal than by baring it in public as provocatively as the most private part of one's anatomy? I admired the talent. I admired the ambition, however much I resented having been made complicit in the banality of such a scene of domestic violence.

No, Maestro Pan Fleet does not take direction well. Had I not been rendered a mere prop for the effect that Sigrid elicited from her gaping spouse? Yet who could deny the dramatic effect?

But was Sigrid's feat of incarnating her husband's mistress so vivaciously before him an action or an act? Did the re-enactment of Siri's brilliantly knotty portrayal of *The Woman Who Untied Herself* – so well received by the critics by contrast with the denunciations rained upon the "hideously self-parodying writer-director" – have a double meaning? Could Sigrid have performed

Siri's performance not only to conjure her husband's shame but to embody my awareness of what she might be capable of enacting in Siri's stead?

***

So when Todorow tells me that his wife *will not stand for it* if he cannot persuade the renowned director friend to permit her to *stand in*, I know what he means, having sweated her performance in the fevered inner precincts of the Todorow Playhouse. But I cannot help him. I still refuse to consider that Sigrid might be Siri's understudy for *KKK*, as we are now referring to the new project. I cannot be his expiator.

"Even if she'll make my life a merry hell?"

"Hell is a setting, too."

Scene 13: Drawing Room

A drawing room. The wall facing the audience is roughly sketched in trompe l'oeil: crowded bookcases flanking an extravagantly draped window. A bull-horned Victorian gramophone is perched on a claw-footed side table. A black chesterfield sofa, planted in front of the wall of bookcases, is faced obliquely by two bright red leather club chairs.

Balustrade, in butler's livery, enters from stage left. He seats himself emphatically upon the chesterfield, leans back, interlacing his fingers loosely about one knee. He has crossed his legs. The noise of a lively party is audible from offstage right.

Lawrence and Jerome, formally attired, enter through the open door, accompanied by an increase in the volume of the offstage hubbub. The sound of a door shutting silences the room.

BALUSTRADE: My dear boys.

JEROME: You've been waiting.

LAWRENCE: We intended to be on time but the girls were so adoring.

He paces back and forth just behind the footlights.

JEROME: *Seating himself in one of the club chairs.* Not

what he wants to hear, I warrant. Listen here, let's just get on with it, eh?

Balustrade does not move. His face is expressionless.

LAWRENCE: The girls can hang upon one so. Natalie and Delphine are the worst. Well, Natalie.

Balustrade's face tightens. He is looking past the two club chairs at Lawrence, now kneeling and fiddling with a shoelace. But Balustrade might be mistaken for peering into the audience. He stands up and pushes past Jerome's attempt to calm him and urge him back to his seat.

LAWRENCE: *Now standing in Balustrade's path.* I don't mean to insult you, sir. I do assure you. It's just that, well, you should know how the girls do hang upon one so. It is enchanting, to be sure. And so that's why we're tardy. We've been enchanted.

Balustrade, still bearing down on Lawrence, casts a fleeting glance over his shoulder and points at Jerome, who re-seats himself. Balustrade, now looking at Lawrence – whose back is to the audience – straight in the face, takes Lawrence's hand as if he were a helpless invalid and leads him to the unoccupied club chair. He presses his full weight down on the younger man's shoulders until Lawrence is seated, too. Balustrade returns to the chesterfield. Sits.

BALUSTRADE: Well, we're all together now. What else could matter?

LAWRENCE: By the way, I've sent for the real butler to bring us something to toast with.

BALUSTRADE: Brilliant.

JEROME: *Gestures towards Lawrence with a tight fist.* We're all together in what we planned. That's the thing, eh?

The butler enters bearing a silver tray of cocktails. Lawrence puts out a foot to trip him, but Jerome swats Lawrence's thigh away, just a step ahead of the butler. Each man is served. The butler, with a nod to his charges, exits stage right.

Balustrade makes a ceremonious gesture while raising his glass.

BALUSTRADE: So, we are ready, are we not? So we know what we are about, do we? I don't believe it. I need to tell you something you may not have conceived of in the imagining of what we embark on here. You might think that the human voice box is a delicate mechanism under the crushing force of your concerted thumbs. But consider this: the master of the house has a voice every bit as hefty his girth. It will take more strength than you fancy.
   Balustrade hands his cocktail glass to Jerome.
   Now, look at my hands.
   Wipes one hand across his breast as if he were using a towel.

Brawny enough, I think you'd say. Healthy nails. Sturdy with the blood that gives them such a lustrous shine. And mind the knuckles: real nutcrackers, right?

Balustrade is now circling Lawrence's club chair.

Sure, I've wrung a cat's neck with one hand. Well this time I'll not take any chances. Two hands are essential. Like so.

He snaps Lawrence's neck.

"Oh no, my time in the soaps was cleansing. I am made of soap. And everyone who touches me is washed clean," chirps Siri in response to the interviewer's question, so ripe with condescension.

He had expected, even wanted her, to show embarrassment for her former life, before she stepped out of the snowy ether of the tv screen onto the sturdier platform of my earliest stage production. I could see the interviewer's question dissolving in his eyes like so much soap powder.

"Then I must ask: What is the essence of the actor, as you have experienced her?" Summoning his answer with such face-saving pretentiousness that I expected him to touch his cheek where the make-up might run.

To her credit, Siri's finely-honed scruple of craft is never to speak unmockingly of her profession.

"*She* is most essential when she knows she's an ignoramus," Siri quipped, flipping a rose-colored suede loafer into the air and catching it in front of the interviewer's nose before he could so much as blink.

She never even left her seat. As I instructed her. Acting or knowing? Take your pick, you can't have both. Me she took seriously.

Hadn't I been the one to prick the soap bubble on its enviable rise, when the slender and fair-skinned – as though scrubbed to translucence by the advertisers' own products – ingénue could have floated away from the theater, the serious theater, on television airwaves limned with gold?

I watched, for the first time – on the advice of a friend, a shameless producer – what we now fondly call

Horror Soaps, in the lascivious flush of their early success in conquering the daytime schedule. What caught me by surprise was the way Siri wore her furiously starched nurse's uniform, as though *she* were *its* attire.

Tuesdays at two. *The Fire in Nurse Fever*.

Gretchen Fever was Grant Park Memorial Hospital's most regimented guardian of the sickbed. Scourge of the wards. Despised by her white sisters for her steely adherence to hospital rules and the fervid zeal with which she denounced offenders to her staff superiors.

By day.

By night, Nurse Fever was the nymphomaniacal succubus haunting the underground, long-abandoned surgical rooms of the hospital's ghostly past. As the story went, it had been a medical prison for President Lincoln's Union Army. Doctors, the walking dead, cruised the moldering corridors in search of the whitest body that ever had writhed in the dark. She was an elusive hauntress.

But Nurse Fever was the familiar of the head surgeon, Dr Solfried.

His actual name was, curiously, the same in the program credits that swept by after the last commercial break.

Dr Solfried was, of course, a spirit whom Nurse Fever passed through as though donning a surgical smock, to perform, in the semblance of Dr Solfried's body, the most monstrous perversions of medical practice. She entered his body at the spirit's behest, that the most abominable medical designs approved for afternoon viewing might be made substantial in the abdominal cavity of the man on the gurney. Some trick of the camera made Nurse Fever's physique appear as a hazy skeleton animating the doctor's translucent limbs, as he reached for the bone saw, the small-toothed scalpel, the rusty clamp, the hammer, the dripping spleen.

I learned only very belatedly how this Solfried, whose flesh Nurse Fever gave shape to in the daily episodes, was in real life the animating spirit of Siri's more palpably penetrable flesh. He turned out to be the secret spouse.

On the screen, the viewer had to take it on faith that Dr Solfried was the eternal mate of Siri's most haunting desires. The reality, if the title *doctor* could be dispensed with, required no such leap of faith.

The transubstantial antics that went by the name of the genre *Horror Soap* were underwritten by clean skin. The program was sponsored by a varied opera chorus of actual soap manufacturers: rose-scented bath soaps, flesh-colored hand soaps, green germicides dispensable from a pump mechanism, vaporous vaginal douches that sprayed a pink tint in the air when squeezed. The viewer, basking in the light of the television screen, was invited to try them all. Only step closer to the screen and it gives a cleansing sheen to your extended arm.

Well, the program was listed in the newspaper schedules as a soap opera with "genre bending" ambitions. But no one was more ambitious than Siri. I recognized it. Yes, I recognized her. The actress herself.

When she answered my call for an audition, making her cagey entrance from the theater lobby, I watched her succumb to the crimson-carpeted slope of the orchestra aisle as if it were Cinderella's slipper. I had the instep of her in an instant. Hadn't I already recognized her talents, invisible though they would have been to anyone else, in the naked antics of Nurse Fever? Not that Gretchen Fever was ever nude on the tube, but she denuded herself of artifice. Such was Siri's most teasing ability.

Wasn't the interviewer a tease in his own right to purr the next question?

"When did you know that the stage was your life's true *manse*?"

"When Pan Fleet took a chance with me and cast me in *The Woman Who Untied Herself*. Could I be that woman, I wondered? Pan Fleet made it so. So ..."

I asked that she read her audition lines – I don't recall from what play – with an accent that would be recognizably fake. Any language she fancied. She did, as you can imagine. None of us seated in the dark abyss below the footlights had any idea what language it was.

The role I had in mind was specially crafted for her, of course, though I had shared that intimate fact with neither my financial backers nor my family of collaborators.

Rehearsals commenced the following week. The auteur and his protégé were at it tirelessly for two whole months.

Of course the theater has its auteurs!

In any case, Siri never fell behind the pace of my invention. I changed the emotional premise of her character dozens of times. She remained the perfect tuning fork, no matter which note I sounded. And I went up and down the scales like the madman I am caricatured to be. Good for business, that cartoon! And, of course,

Siri understood, well before the others caught on, that the shifting emotional sands her character was forced to tread so sure-footedly were precisely the point and not, as her fellow actors and our less empathetic technical crew believed, just the usual unbearably exasperating and all too uterine contractions of my genius in labor. The character was a multiple personality, after all.

"Then how many women, *my dears*, are you comprised of?" zinged the interviewer, noticeably more aggressive now.

"How far can you count," she swatted back, her eyes jiggling with laughter. "And anyway, it's never a question of how many, is it? It's how *palp-a-ble*. The audience wants a body to hold, you know. Like you."

She held out her hand, pale and slender as an eel, for him to shake.

"Myself, I have nothing to say on the subject of acting."

***

Indefatigably enough, that chap had a final question, even after the slippery handshake. He wanted to know: "What's next for Siri Skoagan? Another collaboration with fleet Pan? Something to make the audiences scratch their wooly heads again? Another laboratory job? Another woman tied in knots? Bring on the sharpest blade you've got, right?"

Siri didn't wince at the contempt stropped on his tongue. She cut him first.

"*Killer Killing Killers*. It's not a working title, bub. So, let me ask you: Which is it? A killer who kills killers? Killers who kill only killers? Or just killers, one after the other? Go figure!"

With a flick of my wrist the screen has gone black.

Scene 5: Greek Temple

Greek columns flank the proscenium opening. The stage is otherwise masked with black velour. Two rows of painted Corinthian columns recede into the distance: a temple. The only other prop is what appears to be a marble altar, square with a voluted surface. The purple-robed high priest stands before it, his feet imposingly elevated upon intricately laced cothurni, facing the audience, with hands raised in a propitiating gesture. His voice, muffled somewhat behind a bulky plaster mask, nonetheless sounds forth.

PRIEST: He has murdered his brother. What is left to him?

The chorus appears in two groupings and from both wings behind the altar.

CHORUS: He is singing the song of death to the woman he would woo. He thinks he is god's nightingale. She will hack away the branch that reaches so close to her balcony.

Agave enters stage right dragging her murdered lover by the hair.

AGAVE: Here is my offering, oh sorrowful, sorry priest, to the gods who are thoughtless of a woman's happiness. I am Climax's victim as much as his brother Ajax is.

Climax enters stage left, bloodied sword in hand, his face likewise steeped in gore.

CLIMAX: If I am brother to the ghastly deed, you, Agave, are its sister – you who could have been my wife. How much better if you had borne little brothers *and sisters* into this now desolated world, if you had wed me instead of drawing my brother Ajax into your sticky embrace. *Now you are only the womb of death!*

Agave falls to her knees so that Ajax's head comes to rest in her lap, raises her face pleadingly towards Climax, tangles her fingers in the long jet locks of Ajax's hair.

CLIMAX: Would you take life if I offered it? Smitten still am I.

AGAVE: Would you were smote, not smitten.

CLIMAX: The sword and I yet embrace.

AGAVE: Would that the gods might consecrate your marriage to that jealous weapon!

Climax approaches the now prostrated figure of the woman. He places one foot between her extended arms as she pounds her fists into the earth.

AGAVE: Ayee!

The warrior bends his knee either to kneel or to strike his blow more forcefully. The sword is raised but not yet aimed. Hovering.

CLIMAX: Beat the earth as much as you want. Beat it halfway to death. My brother will never hear it nor answer the call. Nor even suffer that door to shut upon him. No burial! Ajax must burn and fill the air. The acrid cloud, ascending from the pyre on blackest wings, may yet dry up your tears or peck them from your cheek.

AGAVE: *Drawing a short dagger from her bloody shawl, she plunges it into Climax's exposed foot.* Here you are, fastened to the earth. Now flap your wings and blacken daylight with your hopeless struggle. I am midnight's mistress now.

Climax drops his scepter almost directly into Agave's clutches. The girl leaps to her feet and, with both hands grasping the hilt, drives the blade into Climax's shoulder, sheathing the entire length of it in his torso.

"But really," Siri implored upon completion of the scene we had just rehearsed, "why such unrelenting violence?" Dilating her eyes with inquiry, while standing at the foot of the temple steps, she might have been the oracle of the question she'd posed. How could she be ignorant of the answer, having shared my creative process over the course of so many productions?

So I explained, as patiently as the wick awaits the match, that *the violence in the scene is the scene.*

Having slaughtered her brother-in-law, she had allowed the blade of the sword to retract automatically into its plastic housing. Her partner in the scene rose from the stage and dusted off his denim knees with two clapping strokes. Siri had stropped the blade of her weapon just as vigorously against her straight leg, coaxing its retreat into the plastic housing that was its hilt, still warm in her grip.

"I don't really say anything, do I? Just do the bloody deed. And it all depends on the spring action of the prop. If it is well-oiled ... well, is it? Well oiled? The play, I mean. Or is all this blood-flow yours, from a wound that never heals? Amfortas's wound? So Wagnerian, the splatter you've orchestrated for us."

Was Siri challenging her own sense of personal craft, or was she challenging my writerly, my directorial craftiness. My powers of imagination are so resentfully ballyhooed for the conundrums I "suckle", according to one of my critical midwives.

Was her query also a portent?

I can already hear the critic's clacking cavil before the first sentence of the review is struck against the keyboard: *"Murder after murder after murder. A bloody montage, as meaningful as the bleeding frame of celluloid in the eye of a broken cinema projector. This play is stuck on its sprocket!"*

More violence coming, of that you can be sure.

Well, I don't explain my plays. I see them performed.

The serious play just happens. Like murder. A deep enough cut. A crushing blow to the skull. Fingers stiffened to the breaking point around the trachea. The sound of a twig underfoot as the pit opens. A needle in the eye. A bullet to the heart. These things happen. The violent act is its own story untold.

I remember it well, my own violent happening.

And yes, as is the case with the serious play, its success depended entirely upon execution. Not to mention the executioner.

***

I had been strolling in the park. Towering in the night sky, my many-storied apartment building shed its light all the way across the street, kindling the iron tips of the park gate: frail wicks. Approaching the park's exit, I was aware of entering the halo of the building, smiling at the reflective glass door still somewhat distantly aglow before me, and the kindness of my doorman, waiting. I hadn't yet passed through the park gate, but I keenly anticipated doing so. Passing from one scene to the next. It is my métier, n'est-ce pas?

So, the arm snagging my neck, dragging me back into the darkness of the park, was a shock. Of a kind that would cause an audience to hunker down comfortably in their seats in anticipation of a suspenseful ride; waiting to see how it would play out. But two more arms, grabbing me by the waist and twisting the bottom half of my body away from the upper, told me I might never be comfortable again. I was in the grip of an octopus intent on drowning me, pulling me under, filling my lungs with an unbreathable deep. I could see my hand disappear under a shimmering surface, like the mast of a sinking schooner.

Into low bushes I crashed. I could smell sodden dirt. Not exactly earth: dog shit in dry leaves, the remains of a fetid cigar, seed husks and insect bodies. My face was mashed into it. I couldn't throw the weight of my attacker off my back. Robbery was my first thought. But his hands were not in my pockets. And again they felt more like tentacles than hands.

Of course there were two of them, one of whom gave off a perfumed scent that stung my eyes with granulated sweetness. The tears came involuntarily, like water from an onion. They knew what they were about. They wanted my clothes. The hairy hand bristling and the glove-smooth hand ... caressing? I felt both, unable to discern how they belonged together.

Yet there was no mistaking that they were laboring together to extract my arms from the sockets of my shirt sleeves, my legs from the tubular sheath of my trousers. The slither of my belt had, of course, already whispered to me how entangled I was with the branched and prickly-leafed darkness. I had been snared like a snuffling pig in the dankest wood. When I felt my underpants twist around my ankles, I understood that I could at any moment become a trussed carcass, strung up by my ankles to bleed.

How to resist?

For a brief moment I managed to turn on my back, flexing to gain leverage against my attackers. But my hands recoiled abruptly from the tip of an invisible blade that, for all I could tell, was swinging blindly in a wide arc, menacing the flimsy tissue of my nakedness, my pink-as-a-pig's-belly nakedness. Was I not set for slaughter?

Yet even while all this was happening, I engaged in contemplative reverie. I am always the director, however baffling the action. If this were better lit, my audience would recognize it as a hunting scene and realize that this prey would not stop struggling until the knife blade was finally plunged deep into its gut. But knife it was not to be.

Well, I would not give up the struggle, even as I anticipated the worst, even as I understood that if I did not resist their renewed efforts to turn me onto my stomach, penetration from behind would be made easier for the male attacker who was already struggling to prise my legs apart. No sooner had I imagined it, than I was the slaughtered pig turned on their spit for the roasting.

The woman, suddenly shimmying up my back – her thighs, naked above her stockings, were as slippery as they were muscular – reached down and caught my head in a turnstile grip. Pulling my face out of the fetid earth and twisting it over my shoulder for a drooling kiss, she wrenched the rest of me into greater compliance with her male cohort's malevolent design. The two moved as a single hermaphroditic creature. As I was opened up from behind with indisputable male force, the woman pressed her breasts against my violently turned face with the deadly hush of two smothering pillows.

Then the penetrating thrust of the wooly satyr at my back was accompanied by the invisible sheen of silkiness, the breathy rise and fall of the woman's buttocks, disarmingly cool as the touch of marble, where she now rode my bucking shoulders. I felt her heels digging into my ribcage, twisted as it was to accommodate the double assault. The attack became all the more gallopingly centaur-like as my mind struggled to fit my pain and humiliation together.

Until it was over.

It was over more quickly than a horse bolting out of the gate. Or so it seemed in the vacancy of the moment, when I realized they had decamped and left me groveling in the intaglio of my ordeal.

A bitter twig lodged in the gutter of my lower jaw reminded me that I had clenched the ecstatic rider's bit in my mouth long enough to be broken. I still felt the spurs of the woman's fury in the saddle between my ribs and hips, and, lower down, I knew that the puddle of blood simmering in my anus would come to a slow boil of pain. Dried leaves in my hair, the smell of clawed earth, the clot of mud obstructing one nostril, made me covetous of the shallow burrow I now feared to leave. Where but here would I ever again be safe? I had begun to embrace the peculiar odor of my fate that made it so convincingly a place from which I would never again see the light. I lay there on my stomach. I turned my body onto one side. As I began to raise myself, my supporting hand slipped from its rough purchase on the ground. I felt as though I had delved deeply into another animal's burrow. My nostrils were assailed by an atavistic stench. My hand skittered across the declivity into which my belly had been forced. The stickiness between my fingers was furred. I felt the slither of a bony tail across my palm. Yes, what made the monstrous amorousness I'd endured even worse was that my mattress had been a deliquescent rodent.

And then I was found.

As I wriggled away in disgust from the puddled vermin, I thrust my feet and legs out from the underbrush, causing my would-be rescuers to stumble. They had strayed from the well-lit path leading to the park gate. Perhaps they were sniffing out a burrow of their own.

Two smiling faces hovered like moons in the air above me. I had to ask myself: Why were they here on this errant path, at this depraved hour? Was it depraved? How would I possibly reckon the time?

They must be lovers, I thought. Strolling lovers. Now, perhaps all too enthusiastically, they were embracing me.

"Not again!" I should have protested. But I craved the warmth of their bodies and nestled desperately into the caressing moment, lapping the milky kindness of their speech like the cat taken in from the street. They fairly carried me into the moth-agitated aura of one of the ornate cast iron lamps that lined the public pathways of the park.

"Are you able to walk?" Was I? I put my hands to their lips in answer to their question. I needed a physical grip on those words before I could hoist my upper body into the chilly cloak of the air, rustling it sufficiently to show I was, though I wasn't, unharmed.

But naked. The frosty damp smote my reddening flanks and poked the blue bulbs of my genitalia. In the glare of the streetlamp, the colors were dazzling. I raised myself to my full height in a show of strength. Was there to be no end of battling? I shivered warmth, one pulse-beat at a time, from my innards to my flaccid extremities. I felt my lungs fill with air. A breeze feathered between my legs.

It was as though at last my head broke the surface of the murky lagoon in which I had endured my green and froggy vision. Hadn't all my suffering occurred under a scummy surface? I gulped the air even more thirstily. I was a throbbing tadpole impatient to become the frog. The gentleness with which my two rescuing lovers draped my arms around their necks and took my hands in theirs, aroused the thought that the frog might be a prince again.

Then everything around me seemed to metamorphose. When I turned to my male rescuer – had he said his name was Victoire? – I saw him putting a small device to his ear.

"Calling the police," explained his lover – Victoria, is it possible? – whose tight leather skirt appeared, when I turned towards her, to be rent by an alabaster hip bone as if through ruptured skin. And how could I not have observed how Victoire's leather duster was scarred with as many scratches as were to be had in the bower of brambles from which he and his accomplice had rescued me? Rescued? But my senses were weak. My feet dragged between Victoire and Victoria as we approached the park gate.

On passing through it, we were blinded by the lights of the squad car blocking our exit and deafened by its siren's pulsing shriek. The doors swung out from the body of the vehicle like guns drawn for a showdown.

Of the three men who exited the vehicle, and who now stood guard by the squad car doors, the tallest wore no uniform. As he strode briskly towards us, the hem of his trench coat, flapping against his legs, made him appear to have wings. The coat, open to the night air, revealed a lustrous blackness within, as tight and sleek as the body of a digger wasp. The telltale white smears upon his cheekbones, the ruby lips that he had forgotten to blot in his haste to arrive at the crime scene, made sudden comical sense of the fact that he sported an *artiste's* leotard under his detective guise.

Yes, this was obviously the lithe and limber physique of a mime in training. He must have dashed straight from the studio. A mime in his spare time. What other explanation could there be?

The words that burst from the detective's lips were therefore rather startling, as startling as my recognition that this oath-bound upholder of justice was a performer after my own heart. The words themselves were disappointing, however: a pro forma pronouncement of his name and precinct number.

The scandal of the speaking mime! His words shattered the beatific aura of my escorts, fully illuminated as they were in the glare of the squad car's headlights. Victoria's all-too-visibly ripped skirt, and the scarred leather duster of Victoire, caused me to blurt out the no-less-scandalous words: "They attacked me, these two!"

Hadn't I almost wept to be so swaddled in their loving embrace?

I could see they were stricken. Mouths agape. Eyes brimming. Hands gesticulating against my accusation, miming their innocence. They appeared to me now as unforgivably guilty. I noticed in Victoire's exculpating smile a rot-blackened tooth. He was no doubt about to plead his case to the detective. Then, with a wink in my direction, he thought better of it. Instead, he shoved me into the law enforcer's arms and we fell to the ground. Wresting the leather dossier from Victoria's clutches – I only now recalled I had been carrying it under my arm when I entered the park – Victoire turned hard on his heel and sped off. He shimmered into darkness, a darkness that now completely obscured the muddy path into the park upon which our footprints glistened like moonlight on water. In a flicker of inattentiveness, Victoria set off after him.

The dossier! The script!

Hadn't my impatience to put my freshest thoughts about the play's violent trajectory onto paper impelled me to take a short cut through the park? Now the script was in the claw-like grip of a villain who knew as much about violence as I had planned to pack into the many yet unwritten scenes. He had absconded with the eight or ten roughly drafted pages of the new play. But if I could reconstruct them in the fevered hours ahead of me, perhaps Victoire would be the unwitting co-author of what I might now write, vested as I was with the unchallengeable authority of all I had suffered at his hands. My powers of imagination, not to mention composition, would run neck and neck with Victoire's flight from the law. Wherever my powers of imagination would lead me, I knew the path was true.

To the mime-detective I was now mute.

***

"The violence in the scene *is* the scene."

Would this riposte to Siri's challenge satisfy? I really couldn't say. But before she could part her lips, her partner in the scene – fully recovered from his wound – rising from the floor and giving, as I mentioned a little earlier, his denim flanks a good dusting down, interposed himself. He stepped one temple step up towards me, where I stood in the shadow of a plaster Corinthian column, and repeated Siri's challenging words:

"Why such unrelenting violence?"

I had written this young man into his grave, there to stay. But now he was thrusting his chin at me with the élan of a fencing master.

I do not parry!

Knowing how uncertainly his feet were planted on the temple step below me, I merely commanded him to step away, upon which he tumbled over backwards. The crack of his skull was amplified hugely in the silence. The bust of Sophocles he had struck – we had agreed to strike it from the set as too flimsy an irony – was of cast iron.

Scene 12: Bathroom

Vidallia, reclining in a tub, takes sips from a glass that she can pick up and put down upon the silver spanner-tray set before her. The tub is steaming.

Savannah is shaving her left leg in front of a mahogany-framed floor mirror. Its opaque wooden frame faces the audience, obscuring the upper half of her body. She has in her grasp the ivory handle of a man's straight razor. Only one nude leg and her assiduously working hand and arm are visible.

VIDALLIA: Child, child, child. You are a crime against nature, if I'm any judge.

SAVANNAH: Why, Mama, you do love me, don't you? The monster-maker loves her frisky little monster, surely. And here I am shedding my scales so that not one of your party guests will flinch from the fangs I will bare when I smile tonight. Feel how smooth?

She proffers her leg, her foot tickling the martini glass and coming to rest where the tray hugs the rolled edge of the tub.

The dramaturg enters stage left carrying a cane chair. He pirouettes to settle it in the space between the tub and the mirror, giving himself precisely the view that the audience is denied. He releases his grip on the chair. His freed hand makes a graceful arc in the air. He sits, crosses his legs, leans back and extracts a tightly rolled script from within his houndstooth jacket.

DRAMATURG: I've been wondering what that means: "Feel how smooth?"

VIDALLIA: *Ignoring the dramaturg.* I feel no shame in telling you that it is, of course, me you feel, dear one. Think back to your birth and imagine the slipperiness with which you made your way into the world. Don't tell me you don't harbor the creamy sensations of my uterus in those exploratory fingers of yours. That's right, honey-lamb, memory can be squeamish-making, especially when the memory still adheres to your dear mama's most delicate parts. Touch your leg and you feel my birthing flesh.

SAVANNAH: Don't try to inveigle me back into your womb, Mother. I'm running my hand up my own leg, thank you. I'll find myself fine. Don't shake your head about it.

DRAMATURG: Can we stop for a word?

SAVANNAH: *Brandishing the blade from behind the mirror.* Another word from you and I'll slice your soft parts so thin they'll melt between your fingers!

VIDALLIA: Child, I do marvel at how you know your way to a man's heart. Rake back the skin. Snap the elastic of those pectoral muscles. Splinter a rib. Slosh those lungs aside. I do hope you'll be kind this evening. I've invited Jep Dollop. He was a swimmer at the Citadel. Such a broad, blond chest; even you admired it in high school. So do try to keep your vivisectionist impulses under control this evening.

DRAMATURG: I'd say the mother's ferocity is not yet a match for that of the daughter. And let's not forget how the dowager's nudity is her most brutal weapon. Merciless. So let's not be shy of a sagging tit that – as the audience may well recall – suckled her snakelet.

SAVANNAH: Snakes don't brood. Though you might check your trousers for the exception.
She then resumes her dialogue:
Why, mother, as you're well aware everyone comes to your soirées because they know the blood is already in the bourbon and water. Whoever accused you of failing to quench a neighborly thirst? *Turning a smirk in the direction of the tub, her head visible from the neck up, just on the mirror's edge, Savannah nicks her shin with the razor.*
Take my heart away! See what you've made me do?

VIDALLIA: Bring it here, darling, and I'll give it a quick lick. We're like that, aren't we? I reckon I'll be whelping you forever, such is my fate. Bring it here, my lovely, I'm slavering for it. Let me show how much mama loves you!

Vidallia turns toward the dramaturg.

Like that?

The dramaturg nods, smiles.

SAVANNAH: No, mama, like this.

She steps from behind the mirror, all enraged nudity, and with one stroke of her hand slashes a ribbon of blood across the dramaturg's throat.

Laughter off stage right.

Laughter again.

Dr Todorow's face glistened over a platter of oil-enameled baby artichokes. The glaze on the artichokes cast a green tint over his features. He might have been a creature of the same sauté pan. What color would have been better proof of the flame that had roiled beneath my speech?

Furio, our devoted *cameriere*, had proffered those green nuggets of the season on his passage to another table, whose diners, blessed with exquisite taste, had ordered this delicacy ahead of us. His platter-bearing hand had hovered briefly above the floral centerpiece that lay between us, causing us to lift our noses from our menus. How could we not order it for ourselves?

But neither of us was eating, now that the words were out of my mouth.

I hoped I had stamped hard enough upon Frau Todorow's crystalline fantasy of herself – Sigrid as Siri's understudy – that he might see the futility of trying to glue the shards back together. The penitent husband must see the futility of pursuing the subject.

The injured wife had auditioned her revenge plot against her husband earlier this morning in the bedroom set of the Todorow Playhouse. She had calmly explained all. Dr Todorow had substituted Siri for herself on the apparently revolving stage of the marriage bed. The wronged spouse might then seek recompense by standing in for her substitute. She had always dreamed of performing. Why not allow her to stand in for Siri's professional pretense of being someone else on the stage? The role of the understudy appealed to Sigrid. Playing a player. It would be a start. Perhaps of a career.

But the husband must broker the arrangement with

his renowned but notoriously and autocratically temperamental theatrical friend, whatever fracture in their friendship this might entail. Wouldn't burdening him with the risk be the least revenge a wife might wreak upon her philandering spouse?

Well, from my point of view, the audition was done. There would be no call backs.

The dear artistic friend of whom one might believe one could ask anything, the theatrical producer renowned for making anything happen, remained ill-disposed to the idea.

My mind could not entertain the specter of the hoydenish understudy waiting frantically in the corridor through which the actors entered and exited the scenery, expectant of the sound of phlegm in Siri's voice, vigilant for signs of the feverish cheek and cold sweating collapse that might herald the call for the understudy to appear onstage in the role in which she had cast herself. Sigrid preying on Siri's performance? No. Absolutely not. My judgment was final.

Did I dare look up? Should I raise a benedictory glass, dare the doctor to challenge my decision and resume our superficial cordiality? Would he revert to his ebullient self, protected by the carapace of his renowned medical prowess? Or would he dash the hand-blown goblet to the floor in the manner of an offended duelist?

Yes, shards again.

When I raised my wine glass, peering nervously over its rim, I could see the surgeon's own resolve. The beading concentration turned his pupils into magnifying lenses on struts. He might as well have been laboring at his hospital carving table, his hands dredging through arterial blood to find a slippery tube-end of the arterial system. The tremor in his fingertips was obvious as he stabbed an artichoke with his fork.

Like the actor who waits for applause in ever-more-deafening silence, I understood that I had not won safe passage from the conflict. The drizzling artichoke remained impaled on Todorow's fork, a prop for scrutiny, a sign between us that digestion would not begin until the doctor had formulated a prognosis for my intransigence. At once I felt my hospital gown luffing behind me in a breeze of embarrassment. The moment was perfectly antiseptic. The walls of my hearing were white with expectation. Without anesthetic, I awaited the touch of cold steel that would initiate the procedure. I was the patient patient.

Thus did we assume our familiar roles, acting our well-rehearsed parts. The etiology of our collaboration remains a mystery. The doctor is always the presumptive authority, a trusted life-giver whatever else he dabbles in. The patient is, of course, not to be trusted with anything but the thump of his pulse. The key to his character is "the child at play".

Hoping to free myself from the web of Todorow's spider gaze, I glanced towards an adjacent table where a happenstance was in progress.

Only now did I hear what the entire restaurant had surely been attending to for several ever-more-voluble minutes – the final incendiary volley of a woman's imprecations against a man with a scornful grin on his face, a man who, sitting opposite her, was in all probability her husband: "Faggot, liar, prick-slut pig!" She looked at her raised arm as though painfully aware that her final turds had been flung.

As I said, the couple was seated not opposite but adjacent to us. They were meant to be sharing a baked dessert, which the waiter had just set aflame between them. This special-effects man did not know how well timed his effect was, for the woman's raised hand was not empty. She flourished a flickeringly iridescent blue napkin over her head. Perhaps that, and the thought of her own red hair, and the fever she felt rising in her face, were all the suggestion she needed.

No sooner had the corner of the napkin kissed the apex of the flame than it landed upon the husband's shirt front, licking it into full conflagration. The wife's eyes were ecstatic. Her empty hand was a white dove hovering in the air upon which the flame was so greedily nourishing itself.

Or was she waving goodbye? The smile on her face wriggled through a veil of heat.

Because there was a doctor in the house, Todorow's sudden appearance within the frame of action should have been expected. His hand upon a corner of the tablecloth was not. But with a suavity that would have befitted a top-hatted illusionist in the act of revealing a disappearance, Todorow whipped the tablecloth out from under an array of plates, glassware, cutlery, miraculously upsetting none of them, and wrapped the husband's head in the tightly drawn folds of the material.

The outline of the husband's face was sharpened by the sucking breath, drawing taut the tablecloth over his mouth. By now his head was in Todorow's lap, and the doctor himself was sitting, legs outstretched, on the floor. Amidst the husband's tearing eyes and coughing fit, I could not resist joining the restaurant clientele in applauding Todorow's feat.

When he was confident of having stifled the flame, and as the husband's breath heaved strenuously against the membrane of the tablecloth, the heroically attending physician relaxed his grip. With tentative fingers he began the delicate task of unpeeling the mask from the patient's face. Chary of the visage that was surely imprinted upon the inner surface of the shroud, Todorow tightly rolled the material of the tablecloth between thumb and forefinger as delicately as a man with a full belly fondling his after-dinner cigar.

The moans of the husband, whose head remained cradled in the doctor's lap, would have been satisfaction enough for our pitying gaze, had we not witnessed the sudden thrust of the wife's knife-wielding hand. She seemed to have stabbed at the good doctor's thigh, where he pinioned the patient's writhing torso.

Had the enraged woman missed the mark of her husband's abdomen, or had she struck precisely where she intended to strike? She was restrained before a second stab of the blade could provide an answer to that question.

The epithets still flying from her tongue brought a blush to the two musclemen who managed to subdue her only by sitting athwart her legs and chest. Blood ran from the wrist of one of them. She had silenced herself by taking a ravenous bite. I could not have been the only one in that uproarious dining room who wished to thrust a fist into her maw. The poor muscleman's silver cuff-linked carpus would have to do.

By this time, the bone of contention that had been warming between Todorow and myself was quite cold. As was the almost untouched plate of artichokes. It would be removed from the table without a word, under Furio's judgmentally furrowed brow, with the same finickiness of fingers with which he might lift something dead by its tail from the middle of the road.

But no one had died here, though three victims lay flat out on the restaurant floor, arrayed as a centerpiece for the diners who were enjoying the buffet of violence that I, who had witnessed it all so dispassionately from my chair, took to be a personal vindication.

A couple of ambulances arrived. A quick change of scenery occurred. Before we could doubt the reality of it, Todorow and I were hustled together into the back of the second emergency vehicle. The first, no doubt, had decamped with the badly burned husband and his wife in handcuffs beside him.

While a medic busily palpated Todorow's wounded thigh, I plucked his feverish hand from the stretcher on which he lay. I'm sure I seemed the epitome of friendship. And as we set out for his very own hospital, under the screeching alarm and flashing lights of the ambulance, I took the opportunity to ask the good doctor whether he thought I might have been proven right by the events of the evening's second act, as it were. Not just about Sigrid's unfitness to understudy for Siri.

"No. Not just about Sigrid. Nor Siri. But right about the play."

Scene 6: White Box

Lights glaring into a white room. Only the seams in the corners of the room reveal enough shadow to limn the three walls, thereby rendering them visible to the audience. A blindingly abstract space for the two actors attired in white cricket flannels.

HO: *Enters stage right.* You've been waiting.

HUM: *Raising himself from the floor where he has been sitting cross-legged, his head hanging dejectedly.* You care!

HO: Only to inconvenience you, I'm afraid. Tardiness is just the start of it.

HUM: Hmm?

HO: Right on time with that witticism, I must say. But see here, I'm in a bit of a zephyr mood right now. Light as a feather, you know. Ready for the breeze to take me. Any direction will do. Ready to be off. There's only one thing that could cause a delay.

HUM: What are you talking about?

HO: Well, you did bring the bat, right? Let's have it, then. Come on, I can't wait all day. Didn't Reginald remind you to bring the bat?

Ho rummages through a white bag lying two steps to

his right, invisible to the audience until this moment, and extracts a cricket bat. He takes the batter's stance and swings the bat through the air.

HUM: I don't have a ball. I forgot the ball.

HO: Well, aren't I dashed? Not in possession of the full shilling, are you? So that's that, then?

HUM: So, what will we do now?

HO: I'll tell you. I'll tell you what. You stand here. *He scratches a mark on the floor with a couple of quick strokes of his foot.* Don't move. Aren't you a lovely wicket! Well let's say this is our popping crease. *He scratches a line on the floor in front of Hum.* And let's say, because it's true, that I am the batter.

Now Ho clasps his hands tightly round the handle of the bat and extends his arms in order to demonstrate the swing he is about to take. He takes a step back, the better to sight an invisible ball. His eyes align with Hum's head.

HO: You know he's waiting for me to come back with the good news. He'll want to hear me say, "It's done, Reg, just like you wanted it done." And that's what I'll be able to tell him. We aim to please Reginald above all else, now don't we? What more is there to life, dear Hum?

Ho's face twists in rage.

Still straight-armed, he swings the bat at Hum's head and the head goes flying into the audience [effects to be worked out].

Laughter off stage right.

"Unrelenting violence, yes. And one egregiously violent act after another," I conceded. "But senseless? ... no. To that charge I will not admit."

I had given Dr Todorow my blessing to take up the duties of our lately invalided dramaturg, shattered as that poor man was after his tumble from the chair in Vidallia's bathroom. But I had not imagined the scene in which I would have to explain myself to him.

Perhaps this was the so-called *unwritten scene*. We tribesmen of the stage speak often of the *unwritten scene* in low voices, shamanizing our machinations with thoughts of what cannot ultimately be realized in the drama, however replete its composition. We often profess that an *unwritten scene* speaks loudly in the enunciated dialogue of the scenes that otherwise only appear to be supremely articulate. But who, even among our ideal audience, has ears sensitive enough to hear this? They exist. We keep faith. It is scripture to us that the script muffles a truth never to be fully spoken. The speech of the characters might tell it to us if the actors are sensitives, sufficiently attuned to the silence they are stifling with their words. The *unwritten scene* is the written scene's shadow. Such are the mysteries we thesps contrive to convince ourselves that we are doing something real.

Well, then. The *unwritten scene* in which I found myself grudgingly cast featured my interrogation by a rebellious dramaturg in the midst of rehearsal. It was undertaken well within the hearing of the entire cast, who were titillated by Todorow's challenge to my authority. No longer scouting their marks, they strayed beyond the stage, blocking into improvisational space.

How had it come about that I was sitting in the auditorium while Todorow was standing onstage, among the actors, herding them with extravagant gestures? He, our stand-in dramaturg, had immediately assumed greater authority than I had granted him. The actors were watching *him* for their cues, not me. He still sported his white coat, the name of the prestigious hospital stitched in crimson over his heart, his own name scripted below that. He might have just come from his rounds. In this getup, imagining that he might never have to shed the therapeutic aura, Todorow had raised himself before me to deliver his denunciation. Did the relatives of his dying patients suffer the same lack of bedside manner?

Standing onstage, he was taller and thinner than ever. He peered down at me. And perhaps because he always seemed to carry about his person a faint whiff of medicinal alcohol, I briefly imagined him as a massive syringe, one to be administered to my ever-more-demonstrably patient self. For a moment I did not know how to act.

Todorow demanded: "What explanation could there be for your relentless abuse of the vitality of these young actors? Their only desire is to bring your work to life, while you mete out death after death to them."

I knew how important it was to interrupt his monologue. A *trompe voix* would suffice.

Though I was sitting in the front row, at the lowest pitch of orchestra seating, I sent my voice high above the scene of our confrontation. I had learned the art of throwing it from a man of my basso stature who used it to gain advantage over men of another octave.

"You should know that I will not defend myself. No explanations! None!"

Well, my voice made mischief, as I'd hoped. Todorow looked up and swiveled his head, trying to locate the voice that seemed to be coming from both above and behind him.

"They call it *throwing the voice*. I can still do it, though few suspect it."

Did I expect applause? Certainly not. Only attention. I sat fast in my seat. I had every intention of being as uncooperative an audience as the cast members who had been recruited to Todorow's cause. I gazed upon them as they gathered like children for a story, dangling their legs over the footlights, hugging their knees, engrossed, to say the least, when I addressed the doctor's complaint.

"You cavil against the murders. Well, what are you complaining about? Weren't you killed in Scene Two – the 'experimental' scene? Or rather, your predecessor was. Killed in the play, I mean. That was my idea. *The dramaturg becomes a character in the dramatic action and meets a violent end.* Clearly it was not the end for you, because there you are, standing here as large as life, inducting us into a new idea of the play. You call it more humane, more moral.

"Let us contemplate your predecessor instead. At present he reclines in his green hospital room, one leg elevated on a braided chrome halyard, both plaster arms extended above his head, as though he had jumped from a high window. His suffering appears to have been staged by the attending medical team to evoke the tipping backwards of his chair, the incident that had launched him off the rehearsal stage onto the concrete slab of the theater floor. That was his ever-so-slightly-comical unrehearsed morgue scene. But not his death. We are meant to see only what we see, if we have the eyes for it. You had the eyes to see an opportunity to replace him. Long live the dramaturg!"

Smiles. I saw smiles. Minute cracks in the faces staring back at me. Melting ice.

"But I ought to tell you more about your predecessor than you already know. And I should also say that the beginning of this unmoralizable tale of Blackout – yes, your predecessor's name was oh-so-improbably but prophetically Leslie Blackout – will prove that all endings are, in the end, just that: unmoralizable.

***

"I've known this fellow, Blackout, since my early days. He was a student lighting assistant. His night job. During daylight hours he labored in studio classes, a fervent acting major. This Blackout was always struggling to pull the loose fabric of his character tighter about him. Nor could he unbutton himself enough that he might step out of the stiff and claustrophobic garb of his own person. He might quite simply have withdrawn from his program of study. Instead, he ducked behind the scenes, to become a student of technical devices. So he scorched his hands nightly, redirecting the spotlight upon the actors who never struggled with their costuming, whose faces beamed back at him what he must have taken to be an ever-more-intensely-focused ray of ridicule. How could he ever find his way into the light?

"So, this Blackout, still nursing his scorched fist, I imagine, enrolled in classes to study the play. The art of the play. No longer an aspiring actor. No longer a perspiring lighting technician. He certainly had no interest in the role of the playwright who, he demurred, can never be sure of what he has written. This Blackout's choice was to become the dramaturg. He imagined the dramaturg as the playwright's oracle, whispering the meaning of the plot as it must play out despite the writer's most delusional intentions, so out of touch, as the writer was, with the practical realities of staging. Furthermore, the playscript is in colloquy with the dramaturg long before any actor starts to lick his lips and prepare to utter the author's lines. The dramaturg has savored the taste of them before the actor consults the recipe. The dramaturg knows what the play means before it may be played with by the most game of directors, actors, set decorators, even lighting technicians.

"And I was the one who rewarded his study. I gave him his first professional role as dramaturg. And I assure you that it is a role no less than that of the costumed players, rouged and made up out of the stories of their characters like so many feathered birds. After all, this Blackout still had the glow of youth upon him. It shone out of him, plunging his former gaffer self into shadow. Would I have hired him otherwise?

"But there is another reason.

"What an idea my young Blackout instigated, with all the insouciance of the ingenue, after weeks of volunteering himself for try-outs, learning to observe us at our work, imagining how the dramaturg might contribute, how he might play his role more obtrusively.

"And so we return to the rehearsal of the bath scene between Savannah and her mother.

"For it was Blackout who boldly proposed that the dramaturg should appear onstage in the newly-written scene. He offered this as an homage to his would-be director. I had already declared my intention to bare the theatrical devices to the glare of the footlights. What are one's privates for, after all, but surprising display?

"Well, what an unexpected exhibitionist our Blackout revealed himself to be.

"And who would have quarreled with him? The scene, which I had thought sufficiently drawn to a point by the promise of Vidallia's nudity behind the floor mirror, would be even more breathtaking if we seated the dramaturg, whom the audience has never seen, onstage, directly blocking the audience's view of Savannah's bathtub. The dramaturg would bring his own chair to the scene as if he were interrupting the scene, just as it was about to bear melodramatic fruit. It would be a bid to unseat the audience with a judicious prick of self-awareness, perhaps already tickling the *tip of the coccyx*.

"That was how Blackout put it himself, and how he put his own coccyx in the wobbly seat of the chair that he envisaged would be the stolid prop of this imaginative confection.

"The dramaturg was, of course, foreknowing about the swift passerine parry of Savannah's silvered plastic blade. He knew that was coming. But he was unaware of the perilous wobble of the lagging rear chair leg, which he had placed too close to the edge of the stage. That was to be the dramaturg's cliff.

"When he snapped his head away from the shadow of Savannah's hand – who would have guessed him to be such a flincher? – his sudden movement carried him over the cliff edge and into the as yet only imaginable laps of the audience, for this was but a rehearsal. A concrete floor broke his fall. Coup de théâtre. Coup indeed!

"So, your predecessor, my dear doctor, turned out to have been more real than even he imagined, as, no doubt, the name on his hospital wristband reminds him all the more painfully.

"*The violence in the scene is the scene.* I do not call what happened to Blackout an accident, a tragedy, a comeuppance, a pratfall, an irony, a trick of fate. What should have been the prick of an idea turned out to be just a prick. Yes, painful. But suffering must be nothing but a scene if it is to be seen for what it is. You demand the dignity of knowing that the anguished cry means something, even if that meaning is coded in the violently spurred heartbeat of another. What I'm asking you to consider is this: What if the dignity of knowing spoils the act of suffering because it is a distraction?

"Ask our Blackout what claw-footed specter pounced upon him on the cleared path of his intention. He cannot say. There are no metaphors for our pain if it is real enough. It stands for itself. Down he went, our Blackout. Nothing but the clattering of the chair in his cracked head. Nothing more to say, not even for the most insightful of dramaturgs.

"Third vertebrae from the brain stem, crushed. A medical fact.

"Even the heroic physician must – I think you would agree – stand impassively at the foot of the hospital bed in professional awe of such violence."

Todorow, still standing tall above my head, perhaps the exact measure of the distance of Blackout's fall from the rehearsal stage to the concrete floor below, now checked the audience – mine, at this point? – for signs of restiveness or seduction. Did he notice that Siri now crouched among them, her eyes just high enough above the other heads as though peering over a precipice. The others, sitting cross-legged, reclining with fingers linked behind their heads, or with legs dangling over the apron of the stage, chins firmly clasped in hand, appeared contemplative.

I hadn't a moment to consider. No luxury of waiting. I had them trapped in the scene no less than if I'd cast a net over them.

"The violence in the scene is the scene. Let me show you that not even violence is what you think it is."

Raising my hand towards Siri, my eyes were at the level of her bare feet where she gripped the biting edge of the stage with her toes. But she met my gaze. I wondered at her easy compliance to bow, then stoop and finally to step down from the stage to the unilluminated mark where I stood between the first aisle seating and the steps up to the performance space. Hadn't her own exasperation at the violence in my play quietly nursed Dr Todorow's complaint? What then prompted her to assist me in my demonstration of the doctor's malpractice? I placed a hand on her hip and danced us both several steps from the stage. One is always better seen at a distance. It is the better scene.

"Violence on the body is an extension of violence in the body."

Siri's flesh-colored leotard – how could she have anticipated its usefulness? – was epithelial in its adherence to her otherwise invisible anatomy, though it revealed her form with an opaque transparency. It was the quintessential prop if I was to expose the atavistic nerve fibers of arousal seething in even the most quiescent body.

"Aren't we made so?"

I wanted my audience to see my hand caressing her waist as a conjuring. Who feels the caress first, the toucher or the touchee? The caressing hand strives to make the question unanswerable.

"When the hand travels, as it is wont, since the skin is a conductor of sensations, one eventually comes to the breast, for example." My hand reached from behind her and followed the sinuous line of her torso from the waist to the pillowy breath of her chest. Siri's right breast fit naturally into the palm of my hand. Then my fingers nuzzled the flesh, still sheathed in the material of the leotard, until I was confident that the material would appear to be rendered utterly transparent, as the friction of my touch slowly brought the aureole and then the nipple into hard relief.

"The body knows itself better than we do. It acts on its own."

Her flesh was still firming up between my fingertips.

"And isn't the hard knuckle of this pugilistic tissue

evidence enough of a violence that doesn't know itself except as some animalistic sense we fear to encounter on the jungle path of our wild desires? Why shouldn't the theater provide some solace on such a lonely path, where at least we have company in the seats to the left and right of us?"

Before I could caution that the solace of *company* was no denial of brute facts, and before I could resound with what was, by now, the mantra of my theory of the play – *the violence in the scene is the scene* – Todorow assailed me from his higher perch on the stage, knocking me flat onto the steep incline of the carpeted aisle. There he straddled me, disadvantaged as I was by the tilt of the floor which put me in ridiculously easy reach of his fists. His knuckles pummeled me. I saw the patient being beaten upon the cushioned incline of his hospital bed. Perversely, Todorow's blows were aimed at my heart. He, the surgeon – certainly not the dramaturg – who had coached the erratic beat of my heart into a life-restoring rhythm all those years ago, now might have been beating it to death. And, dutifully enough, I bled – not from the insult to my unopened chest, but from the back of my head, where he had knocked my consciousness into the last rows of darkness.

Mere minutes later, or so I'm told, when my eyes squinted against the probing light of the doctor's pocket-sized flashlight, his examining face, hovering only inches from my own, shone with contrition.

But did he realize how his violent outburst proved my point?

And even more pointedly, how could I not have

deduced from his calculated act of violence – Todorow had cast himself self-righteously in the role of Siri's rescuer, casting me by default in the role of vilest attacker – that they were indeed lovers?

The clues are easy enough to follow. I know my plot moves.

Scene 11: A Motel Room on the Beach

Man and woman lie across each other, nude. The steel-gray bedsheets are as smooth as the deck of a ship beneath their languorous extremities. The framed canvas mounted over the pickled wood-planked headboard is a seascape. It is so washed with light that the contours of dune and wave are merely latent. The lights from the motel office shine through the black glare of the window.

GERTRUDE: The surf in here is much cleaner and easier to ride. I should wash the sand from between my toes. I hate coming back to dry land. Except for you, of course.

CLAUDIUS: But you are a diver, too. I can testify to that. You know the waters. You are a creature of these waters. And what a creature!

He grabs a foot and licks the instep.

GERTRUDE: And you are a slitherer, my wicked eel.

CLAUDIUS: You have quick enough hands. Nothing to worry about in the deeps of that realm. And you're always ready for a plunge.

The sound of footsteps. A knock on the door jolts them upright.

GERTRUDE: Oh, oh. I know his tread.

As she gathers the sheets about her, Claudius is merci-lessly exposed. Hamlet enters with the "do not disturb" hang tag dangling from gritted teeth. The room key is in one hand, a gun in the other. A snub-nosed pistol. In order to speak, Hamlet lets the hang tag drop.

HAMLET: Think I'm your fish on a line? An eye on each side but can't see what's happening right under my nose?

He puckers his lips.

HAMLET: You got that wrong. I see in a straight line. The target practice helps.

Hamlet points the gun at Gertrude and Claudius. Then he stops. Looks at the audience. Points the pistol at his own temple. Lowers the pistol and aims it at the wall to the right of the seascape. The pistol discharges loudly. A woman's voice cries out. A few beats. What the audi-ence imagines to be the bullet hole in the wall blooms with a pink penumbra.

I hadn't, in the middle of our meal, asked if they were lovers. Said, rather:

"You are all set to perform the surgery?"

The sound of gravel shifting underfoot in Todorow's grunting assent assured me of Siri's betrayal.

I knew it was at Siri's behest that Todorow had agreed to hush the heart murmur in Steiger Solfried's chest, the chest upon which this fading thespian was known to pound out the drumbeat of his self-importance. We both knew that in the days of their soap opera collaboration Siri was Nurse Fever, attendant to all of Solfried's fiendish medical experiments. They practiced their black art in the haunted depths of an unexcavated Yankee medical prison. Upon that ruinous foundation the present-day Grant Park Memorial Hospital bestrode Sixth Avenue. Of course that present day is already long past, reruns notwithstanding. So, Grant Park Memorial Hospital and its denizens are consigned to seasons past in more ways than one.

La Bussa was always bustling on Saturday nights.

More dishes were to come. The present course had whetted our appetite for more. The joint end of a *confit* bone extruded from Todorow's lips. The sheen of his salivations was visible on his fingertips. When he let the bone slip, it sounded its note of gluttony on the finest bone china, notwithstanding the shallow puddle of *l'orange* where it splashed. His tongue could not reach the stray droplet of *l'orange* where it blotched his cheek. He smiled anyway.

"Who said we weren't lovers?" Todorow winked. With an idle finger he smeared the sauce on his cheek and licked the orange tip.

"You didn't ask, directly. But you knew enough to wonder how Siri persuaded me to take the case. You take Solfried's chest cavity for a scene of carnality between Siri and me – bravo! But there have been many such scenes. We are *in medias res*, you might say. Upon which tableau does the curtain of your mind's eyelid rise? Let me envision one for you, since I confess that what you say is true. Let me begin at the beginning …

***

"The setting is the park, months ago. It is still fall, heavy with decay, gaudy to the innocent eye. The bench on which I sit is bristling with splinters. Overexposed to sunlight, the desiccating splinters are needling my thoughts of you, and my painful awareness of how the new production is teetering on the brink of disaster.

"I am staring into the convulsive and bloodshot eyes of an overstuffed piebald bulldog struggling to deposit an iron stool on the path before me. I will not look away to ease the extrusion from his mercilessly kinked bowel. Even dogs can be embarrassed. I have time to dwell here, so I will not release him from my stare. Finally, the unrelieved canine ceases his spasmodic attempts at defecation and drags himself off, an ambulant sack of manure.

"While contemplating the canine's disappointment, I start to wonder if Siri will arrive.

"Instantly, her hand touches my shoulder. She has come from behind. I do not turn around but stare at the unmistakably feathery hand, long-fingered, whiter than my surgical mask, cuticles tinged with a blue mist. I am reminded of Nurse Fever's past life, the one you noticed out of the hyper-attentive corner of your casting eye. I think: she who has scaled the ratings charts of the tv screen is now in my range of reception. The whir of electrons pulses through me with this signal pattern – so she has accepted my invitation.

"And then her smile hovers before me. No need to have turned my head. I know what is possible. She is here. You know the feeling when the appearance is just right, when you can't tell the performance from the act.

"Siri is sleek in her navy-blue bodice, her silver tights and her cardinal-red running shoes. The bodice is, of course, a down vest as tight upon her pink t-shirted torso as her rib cage. The water bottle that is holstered at her waist makes her tipping into my shadow all the more quenching, even as she laps from what is undoubtedly the darker well of my ear.

"'You know what it means that I am here.'

"The words ripple through my consciousness with the knowledge that something is expected of me, too. My own presence is felt so fervently I might be as flush-faced as her running shoes.

"'Give me the cutting hand,' Siri inveigles me. Her breath hangs in the air, a sensuously billowing cloud promising unexpected, perhaps turbulent weather.

"I had expected a tight black leather skirt, slashed up one side. I'd hoped Siri herself might see that the skirt perfectly matched my well-scarred leather duster. My shoulders fit tightly to the weathered stitching around the armholes. It is an embrace that I anticipate might be fitted as well to her cuddlesome shoulders, if I extend my arms.

"But it no longer matters, since the hand that Siri has taken from me is already warming between her legs, which I am keenly aware no passing eye will be able to ignore. The glare of the sun gives precise focus to the warmth of the moment. My hand is the glittering retractor to the deft incision she has made of her thighs. The operation is underway.

"She is squeezing the silver tights together where my hand lies and does not wish for release. Her face feels closer to my lips than my own breath. Out of the corner of one eye, I spy the bulldog again. Having circled back to his sacred ground, he is now shaking off the last teardrop of a laborious excretion. Unleashed from the paroxysms of his sphincter, he jauntily decamps.

"Siri's lips part, proffering words with a livid sheen. Her eyes are tightly shut against the glare. I admit: blades and sutures come handily to mind, even outside the swinging doors of the surgery.

"I hear her speaking before I know what she is saying, like the snap of a latex glove at the wrist before the fingers grip the hilt of the lancet. I know the feeling. I am not being deliberately obtuse. Be kind enough to wait for me to finish, as I waited for her.

"'Want to play?'

"I am not aware of having nodded. I know what she means. But here? Of course not. She has a place in mind. I am happy to be led to the spot. I am a dog led by a compelling scent to private business.

"The gravel shifting underfoot quickens the tidal pull of Siri's grip on my hand.

"I should explain: on weekends I navigate my own yacht with white-capped élan back and forth across the Sound. But even with my feet planted athwart her beam, I have never felt the rising wind in my hair, the slice of the keel between my legs, as I do when Siri lays her hands on my tiller. We are running now, racing ahead of stampeding clouds. The grey dome of our destination is bobbing significantly on the dripping horizon.

"I recognize a granite temple rising above a few foundational tiers of red brick, where one's pathway abruptly forks. You cannot approach the temple steps head on. You must go to the left or to the right.

"I speak of your very own path, my fleet Pan. You know it well. It beckons from the brass-handled glass doors of your apartment building. Cross the street. After you pass through the iron gateway into the park and find yourself straddling a fork in the path, you come upon what is nothing more than a public convenience in the guise of a Greek temple. A pissoir. Men's to the right. Women's to the left. When you arrive at the fork in the path and are uncertain which way to turn, you are of course already endowed with the stance that would serve you well before any of the urinals gurgling within. Take the path to the right. Enter. Passing through the tiled arcade of sinks and urinals, you come to a winding wrought-iron staircase. A sagging chain bars your path. No attendants on duty. Your ears prick to the roiling tides of the sewer system washing up against shoals far beneath you. This is where Siri is leading me.

"With the first thunder-blast overhead, the green iron door to the temple sways under Siri's free hand. Fluorescent light flickers on. The stench of stale urine, suspended in the dampness of the inner sanctum, assails my nostrils and sours my appetite. But she rushes me through the porcelain hall of serried urinals. I tighten my grip upon Siri's hand, only to feel her fingers slipping away. She strides ahead of me into the darkness, one bright bare ankle passing over the swaying iron chain and landing on the first tread of the iron stairway that unwinds beneath her feet. I know I am meant to follow ... and I do.

"Once over the clanky sway of the chain, I find myself tumbling down the coiling stairway, still tethered to Siri's haste, feeling the suction of an invisible drain within the concentric headiness of our descent. The darkness suddenly roars below us. Are we plunging into a river? I fear that the sound of rushing water heralds a drowning depth.

"But a sharp twist in Siri's step jerks us away from the brink. A blinking trail of ceiling lights leads into a tunnel. We rush through the tunnel's menacing slickness, in danger of losing our footing with every step. Then another staircase. Now we are coiling again beneath the last dank landing of the staircase, turning, crouching, kneeling. Siri draws me further down until my face is dripping with mossy dampness exuded by the walls of a natural grotto. Then we burrow into an egg-shaped crevice in the crumbling brickwork. The wall, broken open, is hardly less mysterious than the forced entrance to an Egyptian tomb, and we – we are the wonderous discovery within. We embrace in the closeness of the burial niche.

"'Fuck me! Fuck me hard, deep in my womb!' Siri's words were of sufficient incantatory strength to bring a pharaoh back from the dead.

"*'Fuck me in my wound!'*

"Does it matter that I hear it differently the second time? Our clothes are ripped open. The tremor of desire shreds all obstacles to placing skin on skin. I am soaking in her juices. I am deep within her, deeper than the strangling undertow of the sewer current racing beneath us and roaring in my ears. In the spasm of her embrace, my own mouth is as rigid as the violently yawning lips of a drowning man. I am ecstatic."

I did not respond immediately. Rather, I wished Todorow to imagine that what I had to say to him now might be the unwished-for mouth-to-mouth resuscitation of the happily drowning man. He wishes nothing more than to sink deeper into ecstatic oblivion. I said:

"You probably aren't aware of it, but the 'wound' is what she carries from her days as Nurse Fever. Siri's little joke. You know *Parsifal*? Amfortas's wound? *The womb that will not heal.* We are speaking of an opera after all, however sudsy. In episodes when her duties took her to the obstetrics wing of Grant Park Memorial Hospital, Nurse Fever casually but pointedly substituted one word for the other. A calculated malapropism. It was Siri's coded message to her most loyal, most besotted viewers. The electronic pulse of the televisualized world of Grant Park Memorial Hospital proffered a ready womb for their zygotic imaginings. Could they not then be midwifed into knowing how the womb also wounds? Think only of the insatiable desires that the show's rapacious advertisers inflict upon their viewers. Such was Siri's obstetrical advice to the women nursing their fantasies at home.

"I am in on the joke. Siri's producers and the show's writers were happy to indulge any amendments their star players made to their ludicrous scenarios, so jaded were they with the travesty of their trade. Any semblance of seriousness was, after all, only an act. Every actor knew it.

"And so, a giggle passed between Nurse Fever and Dr Solfried as they crossed the threshold from one set to another. One world to another. After every first commercial break the scene shifted from the sleekly modern glass and steel façade of Grant Park Memorial Hospital, shining with the sobriety of daylight working hours, to the murky basement carved from the foundation of the Union Army Hospital for soldiers whose minds were in delirious flight from the chaos of battlefields. This vampire world came alive only after snowsqualls of flaky laundry detergent, cascades of unfurling rolls of toilet paper, the surging rivers of flower-scented hand lotion that so bracingly *hygenicized* the viewers at home. Only after the second commercial break was Nurse Fever, unbridled of her straitlaced daylight persona, free to become an enthusiastic collaborator in Dr Solfried's black deeds.

"You've watched it, I'm sure. Particularly after the first commercial break, when we could expect to see Nurse Fever corseted in flaming silk, her yellow tresses loosed from the grip of the stiff white cap pinned to her scalp. Her bosom now blooming where formerly the hard bud of her nurse's medallion pin had nipped together the collars of her tunic. Her garters startled the hem of her white skirt. Her lips were as incarnadine as the trim of her bodice. She served the doctor's every desire.

"Dr Solfried took the mind-jangled patients, in their chains, one episode at a time, into his surgery. Cranial saws and drills passed from Nurse Fever's hands to his, auguring lurid violence. And when the patients' torments were over, we peered intently at the screen, as though through a boudoir keyhole, in the hope of catching a glimpse of Nurse Fever's nymphomaniacal debauchery with the depraved doctor. They took their pleasure on the blood-soaked surgical table. Though repeated at the end of every episode, like the refrain of a filthy limerick, it was a scene discreetly shot in the most unilluminating light.

"It was, after all, a late afternoon show, when minors may be watching. Dimness blurred the titillated eye before the last commercial fell like a stifling curtain. The fade to black did not discourage the blank stare into the screen. I speak of the most secretive and lascivious aficionados of the soaps – men like yourself. The knowing housewives would already have switched channels.

"For a general audience, including women and children idling in the late hours of an ordinary weekday afternoon, there can be no consummation of the pornographic tease. A strict code prohibits it. Their decency is at risk. Men like yourself would no doubt prefer a heated view into what you might call Nurse Fever's womb. Instead the camera casts its cold eye on her festering wound, the comparably banal reminder of her vampirism.

"Recall the seminal episode when the doctor begged to drink from the wound pulsing at her neck. Dr Solfried let the words fall prophetically from his lips with a slurping smile: 'Nurse Fever, you will be my salvation.'

"And you, my medical friend – now that you have agreed to perform his surgery – you are meant to be *his* salvation. That's what Siri says."

Scene 7 [out of sequence]

The cloakroom of a noisy restaurant. Tables being announced in the background. There is no one in attendance behind the counter where the numbered 'claims' hang from wooden paneling on a prominent hook. Black numbers on white tiles. The deeply folded crimson curtains into which the custodial attendant is expected to disappear hang limp. Nothing moves.

With darting eyes, his face drained of blood, Marvin, now wigless, with dripping steak knife in hand, and bustling his skirts around a corner of the abandoned counter, dives through the curtains. When he reappears, still wriggling into the bristling fur of his coat, the audience can see that both of his hands are free. Without a further glance over his shoulder, but recklessly unsteady on stiletto heels, he hastily exits the restaurant, stage right.

Invisible behind the set wall, voices cry "Murder!"

When Frau Todorow appeared at my door in violet suede pumps, plush as her footing in the deep mauve pile of the doormat, I concealed my lack of surprise.

Once she had crossed the threshold, I noticed the chiseled intaglio of what must have been her heavy deliberations before touching the bell. Her shoes' indentations, turned every which way in the pile of the doormat, were the ghosts of her decision-making. But here she was, in person. And now, touching my shoulder with one hand to steady herself, she bent one knee then the other to remove her suede pumps and set them aside. The ceremoniousness of the act, as if in accordance with some house rule, as well understood as the hush that greets one in the inner precinct of a temple, for a moment made me wonder where I was.

Fingertips pressed together, palms kissing tenderly, she stood still and lowered her face to mine. She was so much taller than I was.

"I pray you know why I come."

Her eyes appeared to be sewn shut. The lily lids, bunching beneath the suturing lashes, so straight and onyx, made her seem to be watching a bustling scene of action unfold behind them. The mind's cinema undulating in the faint tracery of her capillaries. Perhaps she was conjuring up the scene itself.

Kneeling now in her stockinged feet, her knees sank into a crimson lozenge of my Bokhara carpet. She was knitted up in a severely tailored steel-grey tweed suit, the jacket unfastened to reveal the lace of her slip fluttering underneath. She turned her long white face up to me, eyes shut, lips parted and sheened with the serenity of an antique sculpture.

"I can help you," she said. Words that struck her eyes open.

Those eyes might have been hinged in the head of a wooden doll thrown violently to the ground by a tantrum-stricken child. Now Sigrid was dilating her nostrils. Now she was making a gash of her recently enameled mouth, the corners cut into a grim frown. Her lower lip pouted and trembled. She laughed gaily. She narrowed her gaze. She held the tip of her tongue between her front teeth and let it go, as if it had been ripped from her possession. She went wall-eyed like an epileptic and let her body be possessed by the spasm, which left her at last sprawled and ready for the chalk outline that the attending policeman might trace around her.

My response? I pulled tight the silk belt of my dressing gown, still wrinkled with the contours of the nap from which I had been awakened. Sigrid might have been the residue of an otherwise forgettable dream as I hurried to answer the doorbell. But there was nothing dreamy about her any longer. She had flung icy water into my bleary eyes.

Nonetheless, I was obliged to tell her that her second audition had failed.

How remarkable that, at that very moment, a ray of light splintered from my panoramic window. Its descent between two soaring office buildings pierced her heart as adroitly as the most well-placed spotlight adjusted on the seared palm of Lionel Rimsky, my lighting director. *The Great Rimsky* couldn't have made better iconography of the moment. So, Sigrid's bid for enchantment was renewed. I scanned the occasional tables in my circular entryway for a vase I might crack over her skull, to bring the curtain down. I knew her to be a dangerous woman.

Todorow himself had painted the word picture of her in her office. She was perpetually awaiting the small, delicate, shy child client whom all who knew her knew would never grace her office again. Her reputation had reached the back rows of the audience. She was on no one's list of referrals.

Nonetheless she waited, tapping her patent leather toe beneath the beveled glass of her uncluttered desktop. Posed hieratically against the tall back of her swivel chair, she surveyed the sand-colored walls, raking the sand with her eyes like a Zen gardener, systematically returning to the golden doorknob that closed the circuit of her gaze. Not even the most concentrated twisting of her long white neck could make that knob turn. A few potted plants, their peat-colored leaves crisp with their demise, accentuated the stillness of the décor, in grim counterpoint to the tapping toe.

No longer in the company of a white-coated receptionist, Sigrid waited in her own waiting room the day long. The luminous computer screen, poised for scheduling, demanded the refreshing touch of a fingertip every quarter hour or so, a finger that otherwise tapped a dissonant rhythm on the phone's headset. The phone never rang, but her expectation that it would never wavered. Its ring was already so loud in her head she pressed moist palms to her ears to quell the sound.

At least she was a psychologist, with the means to analyze her predicament.

Had Todorow smiled at his own witticism? Or was the smile meant for me?

I felt like I was standing on the surface of the sun, so powerfully was the entryway of my apartment illuminated. I did not smile. My eyes were haloing with heat. Here, too, sprawled before me on the sharp angles of my Bokhara carpet, Sigrid was waiting. As I watched her skin begin to warm with the honeyed sunlight now coming more thickly through the window, heaving to a fine simmer, I could not prevent myself from swallowing. I knew well enough that she was alert to the slightest response to her performance. Even auditions are performances. And where, more tellingly to discern the tattling tell, than in the carnal protuberance of my Adam's apple? Again, I swallowed, this time with volition, imagining I could render myself unreadable to even the most scrutinizing gaze. I am fiendishly attentive to detail. Even my worst critics say so.

What instant of my inattentiveness allowed Sigrid to take control of the situation? Was it a torpor induced by the sun? "Light holds us all in paralyzing torpor," I should have whispered to myself, to break the spell of Sigrid's seductive luminosity. But, of course, mine was the inattentiveness of the actor fumbling for his line.

"A dangerous woman." Even her knife-wielding husband had confessed it, fearless as he otherwise was under the bright and searing lights of his surgery.

In an instant, the light was as molten as the bubble at the end of a glassmaker's blowpipe. Sigrid moved so abruptly that I felt englobed in the glassmaker's fever dream.

Perhaps my imagination is too vivid. But Sigrid's leap from a supine position at my feet was like the invisible glassblower's shaping breath, elasticizing everything, including myself, in Sigrid's voracious embrace. And yet the intimacy was so scalding I might have sweated her from my own roiling limbs and torso. Did I have to fight her off, or was she also a prisoner of the glassblower's breath?

In the next instant I worried what twisted, brittle figurine might be frozen into perpetuity upon the cooling of these tempestuous elements. All the more reason to stoke the coals hotter. So I took her into my arms and we rolled upon the carpet, turning on the axis of the blowpipe, swelling and puckering until we took the unmistakable form of horse and rider. She rode bareback.

Imagine the shivering withers of the horse, the kick of the rider's heels, the rider's back arched and stiffening against the thrust of her hips, the mane flying into discrete translucent filaments, conjuring the ferocity of the gallop for the admiring eye of the craftsman who would take the glass figurine gingerly on his fingertips to inspect the workmanship. The image fulfilled all of my forebodings.

And there we lay, limbs still throbbing with the struggle that had left us breathless in the softening rays of the afternoon sun. Shards of color, broken from the weave of my Bokhara carpet by the refractive glass of my wraparound apartment window, flickered on the whiteness of Sigrid's naked thigh. Her still half-stockinged other leg stretched languorously, its knee slightly canted and its foot flexing green-enameled toes. Turning my head towards the smoldering recline of her blonde, disheveled head and raggedly clad torso, I reached for the cigarette Sigrid proffered between stiff fingers. Sprawled naked upon my dressing gown, I took my first nicotine puff like a horse pill, or the gulp of ice water that would have loosed it in my esophagus.

No. Like the glassblower unsuckling his artisanship from the tit of the blowpipe – if I may keep my thoughts aglow for one moment more in that ever more fragile conceit – I have little else to explain what had transpired. Ash on my belly. She crushed the butt in a heart-shaped crystal tray.

***

When I announced to the assembled cast of our play that Sigrid would understudy Siri's role, Siri blew a kiss across the rehearsal studio. But something in the atmosphere pulled the wings off it before it had traveled halfway. Our new dramaturg palpably stiffened beside me. His indrawn breath seemed to pull the corners of the white rehearsal space taut, exposing the seams joining one wall to another, revealing the skeleton of the space. The room's dimensions – floor, ceiling, walls, all shockingly white – were fiercely delineated, as straight as punishing rods.

Suddenly, inexplicably, I stood apart like one for whom the whistling rod would be used to make an example.

I assumed Todorow had rushed off to tend to an emergency. Siri had vanished more mysteriously. The others appeared not to have heard my announcement. They milled inaudibly in front of me. Silence emanated from the white surround. To me, these blurry figures groped in the white space of the rehearsal studio as though blinded by the surfeit of reflected light. I was afflicted with their dizziness before the floor hit my head.

When I was brought back to consciousness with the aid of smelling salts, I knew where I was.

Still in rehearsal.

More specifically, I understood that I had lain passively under Sigrid's studious gaze. She sat on the edge of the couch, a blur, awaiting a sign that the sharp edges of my reality had been restored. But at the precise moment when my focus crystalized, she herself appeared lost to distraction, languidly passing the broken vial of smelling salts back and forth under her rhythmically flaring nostrils. She could have been mistaken for an idle shopper sampling perfumes at a department store counter.

Scene 7 [rewrite]

A noisy restaurant. Crimson drapes hang claustro-
phobically on every wall. Klaus and Marvin sit catty-
corner at table. Marvin is wearing a blond wig in a
pageboy cut. Also, a loose-skirted gown with a tight-
fitting velvet jacket that perfectly matches the restau-
rant's drapery. His stiletto heels: crimson. Klaus sports
his navy officer's blue dress uniform.

KLAUS: Is this public enough for you?

MARVIN: For what I have in mind.

KLAUS: You said your mind was a blank. That you only
wanted appearances to show. Nothing but scenery.
That's you, you said. You just wanted to be seen.

MARVIN: You heard me, did you? Wouldn-a-thunk it.
And you, with your medals shimmering against the dark
blue sky. Oh my! Oh my!

KLAUS: But this is my uniform, not my dress. My dress
uniform. It's the real thing, not a costume. I'm the real
thing. Reality is a thing. It's not a show.

Marvin turns a blackening face toward Klaus. With his
left hand he ceremonially removes the wig and vehe-
mently splashes it into Klaus's soup.

MARVIN: Oh, I couldn't agree more.

Marvin steadies the steak knife in his fist and impales Klaus's hand where it rests, palm down, upon the dining table. He is poised to push his chair away from the table. The rest of the restaurant clientele remain oblivious. Marvin stalks off stage left, steak knife in hand.

Offstage laughter.

"Do you *not* expect us to wonder? Scene after scene after scene after scene after scene. Shocking enough to see the first couple of victims keeling over into pools of blood. Worrisome enough that the blood is a slipping hazard onstage. But more hazardous to the actor is the slipping away of any motive that might give the killings a point, especially the killer poised with knife in hand."

Over her shoulder, the letters carved on steep, mirroring bevels into the bronze plaque, reading *Stauffenburg Cardio-Surgical Unit*, appeared to wink at me with a hint of condescension.

Siri had chosen this time and place – hospital, the waiting room – to speak of the very work that Steiger Solfried's surgery was interrupting, even as we awaited the outcome of that gory interruption, enjoying what was, at least up to this moment, an entirely pantomime *entr'acte*.

"Still, someone must be honest with you, my fleet Pan. Endless murdering dulls the mind. You'll have your audience lost in the dead weight of their bodies, falling asleep in their seats."

I stood up, heard the floor wax squeak under the assertive rubber sole of my shoe, and pivoted toward Siri's rigorously sculpted posture of indignation. She sat, arms and legs tightly crossed, visibly pulling the knot tighter against her muscular midriff, staring through me, her eyes following the path of infinitely receding ceiling lights sparkling through the aperture in the door that, all in good time, swings casually open for the surgeon's report to the already grieving family.

"I'm starting to feel sorry for you," were her genuinely mournful words.

"How many of these scenes have you written in your *head*? That's where the problem is, isn't it? The head. Somewhere deep within the moistly parted lobes of your brain you are still conceiving violent acts. Acts without meaning. You are so deeply hidden within yourself that even the deftest reach of your legendary midwifery can't get a forceps grip. It all comes headfirst, as your most reliably disparaging critics relish saying of your ever-more-prodigal offspring.

"Well, are you encouraging us to join that critical chorus, even as we take your direction?"

I suddenly wondered at the wide-openness of her eyes, swallowing the barely visible white-gold brows into the bluish folds of the silky eyelids. Her mouth opened, readying itself, I imagined, to take back everything she had spewed at me in a single gulp of contrition. Would that guilty tears might pour forth.

It was not to be. The inexplicably made-up eyes were pushing past me.

Then I heard the swinging door of fate whoosh behind me. Footsteps followed like a drum roll.

Todorow's green operating room clogs suddenly intruded upon the glossy linoleum square on which I had cast my eyes in anticipation of Siri's recantation.

"Success." The word brought him up jauntily beside me, facing Siri for a curtain call. If he were to take a bow, would I applaud? I could only think of the two of us as the frozen masks of comedy and tragedy. His smile, his bravado pronouncement, rendered my scowl a feeble decoration above the proscenium of his proud accomplishment.

Then, with one arm slung loosely round my shoulder, he reached out his other to pluck and kiss the back of Siri's gratefully extended hand. The moist chafing of his rubber glove upon my shoulder conjured the squeamish notion that I had become a hand-sized organ.

"The heart has nothing more to say. The murmur has been silenced." With a marble-eyed glance in my direction, he added: "Would any other plot outcome really have been imaginable, the idle imagination notwithstanding?"

And then the gloves came off in one another's hands. Snap. Snap. Like shriveling condoms or umbilici. Latex does contract so. Not unlike the heart. Systole.

***

I might then have said something to Todorow about the unstoppable murmuring of his own wife's heart while in my bed. So many murmuring hearts in our resoundingly enchambered family drama.

***

Todorow wouldn't have imagined Sigrid cavorting in my bed. For him, she was ever more the stiff and watchful sentry of her empty office. The hands of the wall clock were the only things that moved in the honeyed viscosity of late afternoon sunlight. A patina of dust had already settled upon everything from the months of abandonment. It lightly furred the surface of the receptionist's desk, the phone upright in its black cradle, the snugly wrapped computer keyboard, the back of the receptionist's chair. The dust fogged the aptly themed prints hung on every wall. Scenes of children lashing sailboats to docks, struggling with the leashes of unruly dogs, straining against the flexed length of fishing rods, the heels of their naked feet dug into a riverbank, lifting themselves into trees on vinelike ropes, reaching hands over unfordable streams, the fingers barely touching. Her eyes moved listlessly from one adventure to another without any boisterous eventfulness to break the silence.

Only the words *Dr Sigrid Todorow, Child Psychologist* spoke from the other side of a securely locked door.

How could Todorow have known that the sentry had vacated her post?

***

In my bed, Sigrid shivered the bone-white sheets with the fierce thrust and parry of her limbs. The passionate act transpired in a storm of heavy breathing that verged upon clanking – steel touching steel, panting breast upon panting breast – until the dueling finished and both combatants lay prone and apart, waiting to be carried off by their respective seconds.

Then the heartbeat resumed to the rhythm of her words. Sigrid had at last procured a client adult enough to benefit from her analysis. She had grown impatient with childishness. She would beat the childishness out of me, if she could.

Sigrid clamored to make me know things that she was certain I would otherwise never fathom given the shallowness of my powers of observation. She regularly started by recounting the myriad diagnostics of Siri's *pathological childishness*. I was the presumptively custodial parent.

Had I not noticed the forest of father figures, toppled like trees, in Siri's path? Was I even seeing the forest for the trees?

"She's a saw-toothed ravager."

Emphasizing that she was not given to hasty diagnoses, the doctor's wife assured me that I had been right to think Siri the perfect murderess and muse to my newly confected atrocities for the *KKK* production. But, Sigrid assured me, I did not understand how I was right in that determination.

And did I not wonder at the effusive pretense of mothering that Siri made for all those fathers, myself no less than the actor Solfried, no less than her own prodigal husband? Siri herself had surely been unmothered. The sucking reflex, unrequited in childhood, becomes, Sigrid warned, more fearsome in adulthood. How apt that Siri came to vampirism in her career as a soap artist. A vampire and a nymphomaniac. Insatiably lapping life's shallow saucer of bodily fluids. And had I never contemplated Siri's way of casually tossing a loose shoe into the air? Any excuse to invite an ogle. "The prying eye is caught like a nut that might be cracked in the well-muscled scissoring motion of her legs. The ogling eye, of course, is no moister than the nut where she clenches it."

Yes, Sigrid's nastiness was that eloquent.

"Siri doesn't wear underwear. Don't you know that?" Sigrid winked.

"And now let's consider the *play*-pen you have fashioned for her. What bright and shiny toys of destruction have you not dangled teasingly over the rail of the crib? Pistols, knives, needles, garrotes, daggers, shards of glass, poisons, potions, ropes of various lengths already knotted with nooses, sabers, chains, looming bookcases, flames, razor blades, viciously filed teeth, bricks, truncheons, vials of acid ...

"Rattles to lure the baby. The author rattles his pen. Beware of the baby's reach."

So, one could not say that Sigrid understudied Siri so much as studied her relentlessly. And where there is studiousness there is a lesson; not least Sigrid's conveyance of the fact that Siri, in Norwegian, is the diminutive of Sigrid. Doesn't that mean each is the other's secret?

Even in my bed, the slapping hand of the relentless tutor bringing her inattentive charge back to the lesson, accentuated the clash of our naked bodies. Sigrid's preference in lovemaking was, as I have already revealed, the superior position. She was a bareback rider by nature. But we vied for the position. Eventually, we agreed to share, thrusting and subsiding, side by side, stiff-necked and face-to-face, when we rode the curling foam of my bedsheets like rollicking seahorses. Sigrid knew, of course, the mating habits of seahorses, the family Hippocampus. The male carries the eggs. Womb-bearing incites his aggression. In this way, Sigrid flattered me.

"You must understand that the violent scenes coming one after another in your play, and which the child actress Siri so disparages these days, are the eggs popping the lid of your fertile pouch."

If memory serves – and it does, because of the hip-pocampus firmly lodged in the human brain – I understood her flattery to be a sinister gambit to drag me down into treacherous waters.

When Sigrid left the bed, bending like a swan to collect her garments from below the waterline, I imagined I would, upon her resurfacing, see a festoon of bright green algae dripping from her beak. Beneath the rim of my eye, sight itself bobbed upon a water-world of its own, where my head rolled listlessly in the declivity of the pillow. The depths of this reality we shared were unimaginable.

But today Sigrid merely tossed my own emerald-green briefs at my logy head and snorted. The watery elements subsided. Had I wept? Had I dreamed?

I drew a daubing fist across my field of vision. We were meant to rise early for rehearsal.

**

We arrived at the loading dock entrance to the theater, high as a pier at low tide. The car seemed submerged where we abandoned it below. The tail of the seahorse must have propelled me to the surface. Rising to the air-less platform level on concrete steps, we saw Siri and the other loiterers with parts to play casting black looks at our appearance.

The slap of Siri's open hand across my face stoppered my ears with a rising depth of water. I was caught in a current. I swiveled my gaze and saw Sigrid reaching after me, barely grazing my back with the tips of her fin-

gers that swam dartingly, like a startled school of min-
nows, before my eyes. But the buoyancy was such that I
might have been lying in my own bed, which, upon
reflection, in those murky waters I doubtless was.

"The theater's landlords have locked us out." Water-
deafened, I read Siri's bubbling fish lips perfectly. We
had forfeited an opening date. Contracts had been can-
celed. It had been gossiped that the director had lost his
bearings. Perhaps he had suffered trauma. The script
was still unfinished, adrift, lost to dangerous tides of
authorial self-doubt.

"This show is a runaway barge," Siri bubbled.

Her lips twisted on an invisible hook.

I dug my fins into a palpable current of hostility flow-
ing more rapidly against my breathlessness. My eyes
bulged. The bellowing cheeks of the other actors were
round to bursting. The drowning man must inevitably
become credulous of his gills, as I was. Feathering high
up on my neck, they tickled my earlobes. Before I had
swallowed enough water to become profoundly forgetful
of my lungs, I gave a briny cough.

How could this aquatic conceit be so maniacally self-
perpetuating? One drowns in such excess, I fear. Unless,
of course, one is lucid dreaming...

I awoke in a sweat. Squinting. The morning dew was
already a sticky vapor behind my lids, adhering to the
undilated pupil. A gritty rheum was ground upon the
head of one knuckle where it had rubbed the sleep away.

Sigrid, fresh from her shower, her tight skin still dap-
pled with crystal droplets, brushed a few hard diamonds
to the lacquered oak floorboards, loosed her wet hair

from the turbaned towel, laughed, showing her teeth, and then, tossing her sopping towel over my head, ordered me to "come alive".

***

My vibrating cell phone, calling to me from the floor with an eerie rattling of bones against wood, sent an oddly sepulchral charge through the air. It was Siri, the silently diminutive Sigrid. There was a confused burbling on the other end of the line. The eardrum of the phone filled with tears. I pulled it away from my head to reaffirm the dry touch of my skin, but the voice still poured forth: "Steiger, dearest dear Steiger, Steiger, my beloved ..." was, it seems, dead. Dead of a medical procedure.

Against Todorow's triumphantly therapeutic word, "Success," Solfried's body had hurled a blood clot, horribly besmirching the promise – pure and white as the surgeon's medical gown – that the patient would certainly live.

The voice – if it could be called that – on the other end of the line, no longer able to wring words from tears, was possibly drowning in that extraordinary torrent. Likewise, it occurred to me that at the bottom of such oceanic grief was a question bubbling to the surface for air.

Who was Solfried to Siri, or Siri to Solfried, if she were not only his imaginary nurse?

Scene 3 or 4: Laundry Chute

The waiting room of a metropolitan hospital. The end of a hallway is visible stage right. The letters O-B-G-Y-N stand out from the nearly iridescent orange walls in crisp, steely relief. Each letter is polished to a mirror sheen. Malcolm and Midge, a late-middle-aged couple, are seated alone in two of the multicolored body-contoured plastic chairs that are bonded together in rows spanning the room.

MALCOLM: You say, "unwanted child".

MIDGE: So does your daughter.

MALCOLM: Well, she carried the fleck of light to term for no one else.

MIDGE: Not for you? You persuaded her. Your thieving desire to be the youthful grandfather. You would steal her youth to have her keep the child.

MALCOLM: The child has your nose. What kind of theft do you call that, love? Better to call it inheritance. Family resemblance is a gift, not a theft. *He smiles.* You must take it back. If Sarah won't, we must give it a family. Let's take it. We'll take it back home, nose and all. We will, won't we, love?

MIDGE: Don't give me a reason to think too literally about what a child can steal from a child. Sarah is barely fourteen.

MALCOLM: Nothing is lost when a child is born to a child. Isn't it still just more time, after all? Even childhood is just a passage of time, not the sentimentalist's one and only time. No need to be melodramatic, Midge.

MIDGE: Don't play the hideous philosopher with me! You are the most unnatural father, after all.

MALCOLM: Be honest, love. Isn't it Nature that you most hate now?

A nurse appears from the hallway. She summons them with her hand. The couple rise and follow her into a room off the waiting area. Silence. A baby cries. Other voices mingle. Midge reappears with a pink bundle in her arms. The bundle wails and then stops as Midge quickens the rocking motion of her arms.

MIDGE: A quick promenade with Grandma will do the trick!

She pulls the door closed behind her. The waiting room is empty. Beside the abandoned nurses' station, Midge steps quickly in the direction of what appears to be a laundry chute. A phone rings. She opens the chute and drops the bundle in.

The rented rehearsal space was seldom used these days for finished productions. No longer a working playhouse. What better venue for indulging self-doubt, I thought, as I awaited my troupers in the musty dimness of an auditorium reserved for trying things out.

From where I sat, slouched in a seat in the middle of the fifth row, the red light of the exit sign glared in a corner of my eye. The word gave me pause.

I asked myself: "Can one ever stop writing scenes of suffering?" Only if one could stop imagining.

"Don't they suffer anyway, the audience?" That surly voice of protest ringing in my head echoed the complaints of my cast members. Gaining volume over the recent weeks of rehearsal, did this caviling now command a response?

My disciplining riposte to such complaints will always be: "If my audience comes to the theater to flatter their suffering, why shouldn't I raise a shaming mirror to that pretense? There is no more humanitarian gesture. A conundrum? Not to me.

Yet here before me was a palpable conundrum. I focused my attention on a dramatic scene that was already set onstage. A single ladder-backed wooden chair had clattered to the floor, apparently under someone else's direction. Two squat glasses and a slender bottle, empty, stood upright on a three-legged wooden table. A twelve-inch Fresnel light dangled blackly above the table, its focus blades drooping like bat's wings. The twist of its cable was still unwinding from where it hung, snagged on the iron pipe-grid aloft. Not to clear the rehearsal space for the next scheduled company of performers was highly unprofessional.

A sudden gust of wind from outside the auditorium scattered my thought.

The noisy rehearsal troupe, my actors, bustling in from the lobby, paid no attention to the objects of my somewhat agitated contemplation onstage. Nonchalantly, they skipped down the aisle and lifted themselves with gymnastic ease to the apron. From that low perch they dangled denimed legs or legs in leggings, their boots and tennis shoes kicking. They peered expectantly into the dim well of my seat, where I had sunk low under the weight of wondering what scene of action was set before me on that stage as a direct challenge to my script. I watched and waited for the troupe to wonder with me. Surely they recognized the props on stage to be alien to our rehearsal, out of sync with the lines they had rehearsed. Their obliviousness was unconvincing.

I waited a beat. Would the most innocent-looking member of my troupe hesitantly cast a guilty glance over one shoulder? Were they waiting for me to state the obvious? Would I take their bait? I thought it best to pretend not to have noticed that they had failed to notice.

I quickly stood up so that the troupe would know I intended to get down to business, constrained as we were within the two-hour window of rehearsal time that the surly manager of this venue had allotted us.

On the phone, his allocation of time came with a warning. He had heard rumors. I had still failed to place a completed script into the hands of the producers. I had best wrap it, and soon, he said. The space would not be available for much longer. I should not prevail upon my most influential backers to intervene on my behalf. He would remind my backers that I was unreliable. He would cast doubt on the security of their investments. I asserted, with unapologetic hubris, that my backers would support the enterprise through every uncertainty and delay. They had every confidence that my egg would hatch. They honored my undivinable creative process. Why else would even my harshest critics have taken to calling me "the divine Pan"?

"Down to business, then." I clapped my hands, stepped into the aisle and made my way forward. I accepted a hand-up to the stage. From that vantage I saw, incredibly, that the props – the ladder-backed chair, the three-legged table, the sleek bottle and squat glasses, the dangling Fresnel lamp, the gleaming puddle, all a-clutter in the space of wonderment that was reserved for the labors of our rehearsal – had disappeared.

Had I imagined that clutter? Then how could each object be so distinctly recorded in my memory? Or had my memory fallen under the direction of some malign plotter, the antagonistic scribe of a yet unwritten scene?

That question momentarily distracted me from the multitude of questions buzzing around me now.

Although I had been hauled up to the stage amiably enough, I found myself in the midst of a ferment among the actors. The commotion was as unexpected as landing a foot in a hornet's nest. I felt myself teetering among these would be bacchants. Perhaps they wished to tear me limb from limb. Their voices were sharp and pointed.

One of them took the lead to speak. On his head he still wore the bandage, like a swami's turban, from his knocking heads with Sophocles on the steps of Agave's temple. He declared, with a face as frowning as the Greek mask of tragedy, that they wished to protest.

A protest against *infanticide* itself.

According to some midwife of gossip among their number, I had written such a scene. Set in an OBGYN unit? This was going too far. Murdering innocents. They would not have it.

I admitted that the scene had not yet fully gestated in my mind. Therefore, I refused to belabor the point.

"In any event, this is not the scene to be rehearsed this afternoon," I said.

And, by way of further admonition, I reminded them that we had killed many over the course of our rehearsals. None of them innocents, because we are not entertaining guilty consciences in this work. We are bringing the violent act to consciousness.

After all, what did they imagine we had been doing all these months of gory rehearsal? What could they not expect?

I ordered: "Places!"

Mutiny, or at least melee, was being contemplated. An invisible bellows stoked the already heated air. Voices grew hoarse, limbs gesticulated in protest. The words "too far" assailed my hearing again. Fingers wagged. The words *senseless*, *unconscionable*, even *pervert* whipped the air. Had I been spat upon? Something large and glistening as a bead of sweat shot into the corner of my eye. The eye drooled.

These indignities inspired a perverse calm. With the imprecations still whirring around my head, a thought came to me, slow and deliberate as a chess move, that I required a change of scene. Doesn't a change of scene change the action? I must improvise.

Calmly, I stepped back, folded my legs under me, turning my ankles inward, and peacefully sank beneath the fray. Orderliness is such a calming device. I made my spine as straight as a cobra piped from its basket by an adept charmer. "Eastern conceits," I encouragingly murmured to myself. Tugging at the toes of my shoes, the better to pull tight the knot of my Buddha pose, I snatched a heavy black sweater that had been discarded by one of the overheated bodies agitating around me and bundled it in my arms.

I needed my frenzied bacchants to see how their Dionysian antagonist now reposed behind a Buddha belly of equipoise. I composed the smile of tranquility on my lips. I waited for the inevitable hush. They gathered themselves silently before me, an audience again.

Upon the pout of my lips I cradled an increasingly voluble lullaby, at first little more than a mewling, that I hoped my former besiegers would imagine emanated from the black bundle I had made of the sweater plumped in my rocking arms.

"Infanticide?" I broke the silence that had arrested each grumbling cast member in the cock-eared pose of the listener attending to the faintest of sounds. "I would not choose that word." Another swaying of the bundle in my arms, in recognition of which my ever-more-attentive audience moved closer, slowly, barring their lips with admonitory fingers, peering into the rocking bundle, then querulously into one another's faces. All of them somehow moved as one, first nodding their heads from side to side, crouching low to the lilt of the lullaby, swaying hips. They were as synchronized as a dance troupe, pantomiming their concern for the babe cradled in my arms. Here something new was afoot.

A counter-improvisation! Brilliant. How had they accomplished it? Telepathy came to mind. I thought better of it. But what cunning, what resourcefulness! They must have learned it somewhere, and where indeed but here? I had to beat down the pride swelling in my chest. More important still, I knew I must beat them at this improvisational game we had begun in perfect pantomime and without knowing how any of us would recognize the moment of victory or vanquishment.

I permitted the lullaby to swell on my lips. I was fattening the woolen flesh in the cradle by flexing my forearms, swelling my chest towards intimations of a sucking mouth puckering dryly, noiselessly in the folds of the bundle, as I watched my actors slow the balletic whirl of their attentiveness around me. I thought, incongruously: this is how a helicopter comes to land. They flexed their youthful knees and crouched while surrounding me, offering me no way out of the circle. Unless it would be to board the machine, the blades of which whirred inside my head. Perhaps this was their improvisational conjure: a helicopter. "Bravo!" I muttered.

But no, I understood perfectly well that their slowly rotating encirclement was meant to be a baffle. I could see the faces passing before me, but not having eyes in the back of my head I was unconscious of what circled behind me. More of their shrewd conjuring to parry with. How would I know what was happening behind me unless I turned? How could I turn without wondering what I was turning from?

It was an impossible struggle, to be in two places at once. Mind against body. That was my audition call. I grasped their fanciful conviction that my head was now screwed to my body like the fitting on a plumber's pipe. And the thread of the pipe would certainly be stripped in my frustrated desire to turn one way then the other in order to keep track of their orbit. How would I be saved from myself?

But then, in my moment of helplessness, Siri stepped out of the troupe's encircling choreography, releasing me from my enclosure, proffering an opportunity for me to counter-improvise. If improvisers lose the rhythm of rapport with one another, they find themselves lost and alone. Lovers are bound so. And prisoners.

Thus was I liberated to the next idea. I tossed aside the black bundle, careless of the phantasmal infant's welfare. I rose to my feet. I tweezered the inside of my black pajama blouse – the uniform of my rehearsals these days – and drew it over my head. I willed the loosely knitted v-neck, drawn over my head, to conjure an invagination. And a birth, no less.

And why not?

I emerged bare-chested, excited to be exposing the troupe's frozen stares to a higher body temperature. I unlatched the silver-tongued buckle of my belt and per-mitted my black denim pants to fall with audible weight to the stage floor. I kicked the soft, sueded black loafers into the faces of my audience. I hoped the snappy removal of my scrotum-clutching briefs would make them feel helpless spectators. Was I not newborn to them in my inexplicable nudity?

When I looked down at myself, I saw my naked trunk sprouting from the slack elastic girdles of my argyle socks. A perfect clown's costume. Unintended comedy. Well, the deft improviser must surprise himself before he can expect his audience to bow.

But my audience was not bowed. Nor cowed. And in short order I realized that it was not even my audience – I was theirs. Like the front-row gaper, slack-jawed and glitter-eyed, whose astonishment every actor keeps a covetous eye out for, I felt my own jaw drop. The spectacle of myself I had so shamelessly improvised against their credulity now merely shivered with the cold sweat of embarrassed nudity. It was to them I turned the awestruck gaze of the lucky ticket holder.

Spontaneously, the tight circle of troupers had broken apart like a mouthful of teeth knocked loose by a haymaker. Each member of the troupe spun towards a waiting partner whose feverishly proffered groin was nothing less than the tremulous sniffing of one dog to another. The heads of the dogs locked jaws ferociously. I was caught up in amazement that the improvisation of my own nudity should be trumped by the troupe's balletic improvisation of coitus. Yes, coitus! Their legs were scissoring into one another. And is coitus not what nudity improvises as the best refuge from the blue winds of exposure? Bravo! Bravo! Bravo!

I never applaud. The *bravo* concedes no obsequiousness. But an admirer I found myself to be, in as much as the troupe's improvisational libido proved to be more convincingly libidinous than my own.

Instead of applauding, I latticed my fingers and brought them to my lips. It was a gesture rapturous enough to be mistaken for prayer. Then I gathered up my clothes from the floor and mopped the humility from my brow with a cradled armful of cotton.

The mere thought of how touched I was makes me shiver all over again. But I remind myself that the rehearsal space was unheated.

They lay where they had fallen, like the self-satisfied spent bodies they pretended to be, in a heap on the apron of the stage. Odd that they weren't chilled. But, of course, they were still fully clothed. I dressed myself at once, yet I couldn't shake off the chill.

I had failed to turn on the warming stage lights, which we were nonetheless paying for, so distracted had I been by the now vanished mis-en-scène – toppled chair, table, bottle, glasses – that had greeted me upon my arrival at the hall.

And now I realized there might have been another explanation for the curiously set stage I had so con-foundingly encountered. One or two members of my troupe might have come to the hall before me, to set a plausible scene. Trying to help. The worrisome inconclu-siveness of the script was their inspiration. A toppled chair, a table, a bottle, glasses. Who toppled the chair? How many elbows were balanced on that tabletop? What had been drained from the bottle? Whose lips sipped from the glass? They must already have been in an improvisational mood.

I gave the direction to assemble. I waited on the apron

of the stage for them to gather under my re-appropriated baton, if a pencil rolled upon the tips of one's fingers can be called a baton. I addressed them out of respect for the imaginative vivacity of the moment.

"You want a final scene, an ending to give realistic purpose to our rehearsals. Of course you do. You have waited long enough. And thanks to your improvisational bravura this afternoon, you have earned it! Which one of you was so kind as to envision a final scene set with a three-legged table, a ladder-backed chair, two glasses, a bottle, and a strangled light fixture?"

On their behalf I asked myself: "If one could set a scene that might plausibly be the last scene in the script, wouldn't an opening night be all the more realistically imaginable? Would my young and enthusiastic cast not have imagined it so?" I understood. They looked forward to the reality of a performance. Who would dare to say I cannot comprehend such simple, even practical, not to say merely human desires? I do not plead guilty to artistic effeteness. I permit such a kindness to my collaborators when I can, notwithstanding my uncompromising insistence upon the autonomy of the artist.

Ordinarily, I would have admonished them for their presumptuousness in asking how the play ends.

***

So, did I at last reveal the final and yet unpublished scene, that wrong end of the telescope through which all previous scenes are deemed to be seen properly in the so-called well-made play?

I did. And I requested my cast's visionary complicity.

"See it with me, how I see it. See it from the best seat in the house.

"The audience is facing the fluorescently illumined tiled curvature of a subway stop. Members of the audience who arrived by train bear scuffs on their shoes from the very steps, ascending upstage, that are visible through the iron bars that cut off one's exit from the platform. They are the self-same steps some of them pounded upon while hastening to the ticket window of this theater. The audience members who recognize how we have meticulously replicated the local subway stop may even anticipate ascending those steps on their way home from this performance. But here, facing the deliquescent glare of the tiles, curving over the apron of the stage like a breaking wave, even those audience members will realize that they are far from the turnstile. The ordinarily luminous red-lettered exit signs at the ends of both aisles of the theater have been quenched.

"Peering across the filthy subway platform, the audience will know that from this vantage point they are lashed, so to speak, to the track. That is to say, they will not escape the arrival of the train. They cannot move. The cords binding them do not cut into the flesh and cut off circulation to the feet, as the all-too-familiar cartoon image of the helpless virgin lashed to already vibrating rails urges them to imagine. The cords are burning wheals into the suspenseful brains of the most anxiously attuned members of the audience. If my sound effects are properly cued, already they will hear the grinding wheels of the incoming train.

"The only light in the auditorium radiates from the tiles glistening on the platform wall. And, yes, the tiles are indistinguishable, as no commuter can possibly fail to note, from the nearby dripping porcelain of the urinals that are inaccessible without the key sunk deep in the front pants pocket of the absent kiosk attendant.

"Yes, we have doused the exit signs. But on the lateral walls of the theater we have surreptitiously dropped screens. Each screen is painted with a dusky line of ceiling-mounted fluorescent bulbs, receding into a mock distance of the subway tunnel, burrowing and burrowing.

"There are, of course, passengers. Waiting. Nine or perhaps eleven drowsy loiterers, their shoes gripping the edge of the platform, craning their necks into the path of the train, over the apron of the stage, peering credulously into the painted screens.

"One, in particular, we notice. Slight but tall. He sports a worn leather duster, spider-webbed with cracks. He uses one hand to secure the strap of a short green oxygen tank slung, but slipping, over one stooped shoulder. A clear plastic tube runs from the nozzle of the tank to a fork at his nostrils, where it is hitched up with what looks like a thick rubber band that creases the skin of his forehead. The rest of his head is covered by a paisley bandana. With his free hand he tugs on a blonde goatee. Then one knee thrusts forward, breaking through the loosely drawn line of commuters tapping their toes at the edge of the platform.

"A train rumbles offstage left, building up to a slow roar. Billowing debris storms ahead of the sound.

"Focused, as we are, so distractedly on the broken

line of commuters through which the man wearing the oxygen tank has just forced himself, we almost fail to notice that he has already pushed the missing person.

The oxygen-tank bearer steps into the space he created and stops dead, incriminatingly posed on the platform, right arm thrust forward, legs set apart like those of a runner just off his mark, for what must have been the necessary leverage. The missing person's abrupt plummet from the platform onto the track has not been noticed.

"The screeching whoosh of the train is of course only a sound effect for most of the audience.

"But you still don't see what must be known. The pusher's victim – a stocky, nondescript woman dressed entirely in black, her felt hat flying ahead of her body – has landed in the laps of the front-row ticket holders.

"Yes, the meaning of the play is literally right in their laps, where they've always wanted it to be, like the curl of a cat in cozy flickering firelight.

"Do you understand what I'm saying? The weight of an actor flinging herself from the apron of the stage with the effortless momentum of a child doing a cartwheel, acting as though she has been pushed into the path of the oncoming train, will actually bring the train into the station with eye-popping punctuality for those front-row ticket holders.

"For them, the reverberant landing of the most acrobatic actor among our number will keep the train running. These privileged members of the audience will exit the theater with the train on their lips and forever indelibly in mind. For once in their lives they will leave the theater without leaving the play behind. For the remainder of their so-called real lives they will be able to recount their experience of the play as *something that actually happened to them.* On steel tracks of memory, murmuring with the hazardous electricity of the brain, the train will roll on.

"For the rest of the audience it will, of course, have been just another play."

August 1

Scene 13: Gonzogo's Castle/Poisoned Needle Tip

Imagine Rosalinda's plight. No sooner had Jack's Gonzogo lashed my free hand to a high dowel of the rack, than I felt the whole structure teeter away from the prop wall. The sound of a tooth ratcheted out of its socket echoed in my head. From the corner of one eye I spied the dramaturg taking flight as the shadow of the rack brought a curtain of heavy black bars down on top of the stool on which he was perched.

Jack watched my spread-eagled form hover lazily over him as if I were descending from the apex of a ballerina's feathery leap. Confident of catching me deftly by the waist, Jack held out his arms, as strong enough to cushion my fall as they were to prop up the wooden framework clattering on my back. As I fell forward, he stepped gracefully into the dance.

Except that no sooner had I landed safely in his grip than the prop wall itself collapsed upon the rack to which it had been insecurely anchored. Then Jack was little more than a worse-for-wear mattress, laid flat to cushion a ballerina's practice leaps. He felt the crack in his ribs. A doctor was summoned.

I, the ballerina, was spared.

My long-suffering producers sat big-bellied with expectancy. They were as puffed up as the cushions of the chesterfield that enveloped them. My company of stripe-suited venturers. Or what came more titillatingly to mind: a bevy of pregnant women clutching their bellies, fingering the clock hands of the gestating limbs that roiled within their wombs. The sheened walnut tabletop before them twinkled with its service of freshly poured cocktails, like so many votive candles, as I rose before them to trumpet my announcement.

"We open ..." I gaped at them, dry-mouthed with the realization that they were all but deaf to my words. Challenged by a saxophone's sudden squall of what a card, leaning on an easel by the door, had promised – *live jazz tonight* – I trumpeted louder, steadied by Sigrid's supportive hand in the moist hollow of my back. "We open," I reiterated, "on Thursday, October 18.

"We are in rehearsals. Yes, rehearsals. You have waited patiently for this moment. Come visit. Watch us put the shine on your coin. I think a toast is in order."

Sigrid shone in the light struck from her raised champagne flute. Her platinum coiffure appeared to be electroplated to her head. She rose to her feet with the speed and poise of a silver-helmeted Hermes. My backers leapt from their seats to catch up with her, rushing to chime in with the yet unsounding note of Sigrid's raised glass.

The rousing clink of the toast shattered over Sigrid's closed fist where she had thrust her distinctly unmusical champagne flute too enthusiastically against the other celebrants' glassware. The other glasses remained intact. The solo slivering of Sigrid's champagne flute showered her hand with razor-sharp confetti. Having risen to the occasion, she was now on full display: a conspicuously tall woman corseted in a stiff, high-collared black jacket, partnered with a top hat doffed in her free hand, faun jodhpurs beneath, and all of her, from waist to spurs, realistically muddied from the hunt.

Yes, these were the trappings of Act I, Scene I, with which I had intended to introduce Siri's understudy to the gathered investors. Sigrid had arrived fresh from rehearsals, an irresistible *hors d'oeuvre* of the drama to come. Why else would I have chosen a restaurant to announce our opening date? How else, except by letting my backers each feel a solid footing onstage? Like every enlightened protagonist they must each have their moment of recognition. The imaginative leap their checkbooks had vouchsafed such a long time ago entitled them to stand proud and bask in the glow of the footlights. And a restaurant is a stage, I will not hear otherwise.

I enfolded Sigrid's blood-speckled fist in the matching, merlot-dyed silk handkerchief that had boldly set off the breast pocket of my navy blazer. I had fancied the soft swell of it might even suggest the heave of a full heart – mine, not hers.

Then I couldn't help but envision my investors as a group portrait of well-fed, lace-collared Dutch militia men posing for Hals or Rembrandt. So soberly posed. After standing to honor the disastrous toast, they had reseated themselves along what I was amused to notice was the amphitheatrical contour of our oval walnut table. They grew quiescent, an audience sympathetically intent upon my ministrations to Sigrid, who had made a fainting diva's slow, corkscrew descent into the tufted leather club chair adjacent to my own.

So, patiently staunching the blood that oozed from Sigrid's fingers, I resumed speaking my lines, but now in the intimate, innuendo'd tones of a Shakespearean villain's aside to his unsuspectingly, suddenly complicitous audience. The restaurant's staff bustled about with soft cloths and brooms. A murmur, like a fog of cigarette smoke, settled over the conversations at the bar.

I proceeded. "One caution. The play is, of course, never finished. Neither the script nor – this I promise you! – the production to follow. Anything can still happen. That said, we are scheduled to open and open we will. However sinuously the plotline may coil through this season of rehearsals, we will harvest what we have sown: a marvelous beanstalk. Expect to be surprised by what descends from it."

I would have welcomed smiles. Rather they sat, inert. They appeared already sated with a dinner yet to be served.

When I took Sigrid's hand, to indicate that the business portion of our evening was concluded, I felt the needle point of a glass splinter pierce one of the portentous lines of my palm. Portentous? Only if I were so superstitious a reader.

My backers and I sat silently amongst one another in a torpor of family feeling, like siblings about to broker a donation of blood between them.

***

Until this moment I had not spied the budding adolescent, wearing his father's face shorn of moustache and spectacles. And yet he was old enough to feel the quickening pulse of downy follicles titillating his upper lip. Wearing a duplicate of his father's navy pinstriped suit, the boy, who couldn't have been more than fourteen, had been barely visible, wedged as he was between his father and perhaps his father's father. The two men squeezed the boy against the leather upholstery of the chesterfield no less fiercely than the buttons that held the tufted cushioning in place.

But one of the boy's arms, like a rusty coil sprung loose from the upholstery, as powerfully flexed and as angrily pointed, struck out towards Sigrid with pent-up violence.

The boy shrieked, "Dr Todorow. I know you. You told me that my dog should die."

By now he had freed the other arm and was finding his feet.

The father's clawing hand fell just short of the boy's shoulder, while the boy's frantically clutching fingers laid their sticky mark upon Sigrid's breast. The boy had launched himself across the cocktail table. And though the father's wrathful grip caught fast on the back of his shirt collar and wrenched him into the air as abruptly as the gallows floor falls away beneath the dancing feet of the hanged man, we all saw how the boy's groping fingertips had embossed a nipple upon the front of Sigrid's high-collared shirt, costume fabric being what it is, as thin a disguise as water over stones. Her face was awash with shocked recognition.

Her words were no less aggressive than his. "The boy is oversexed! He was my patient. Lionel, the boy who found his hand in his pants like a lucky charm. When his father caught him in the act, his luck ran out."

As Sigrid shucked off the boy's grip, her breast sprang more nakedly into view. A shred of her badly torn blouse remained clenched in his fingers as he ricocheted back into his father's grip.

The father slammed the boy belly down upon the table. His straight arm was an iron bar forced up against the base of the boy's skull. The boy's face was slapped into harsh profile against the tabletop. Only one terrified blue eye was visible, little more than a rent in the taut, bloodless skin that stretched over the cheekbone. A caterpillar of blood-streaked green snot crawled from one nostril.

Only as the table began to tip over could we see that the father was standing on tiptoe to maintain his iron grip on the child's reddening nape.

When the table's beveled edge clattered at my feet, Sigrid made a strategic leap over it. She had entirely stripped herself of the rag of a blouse that nonetheless, with her fists twisted into the chemise-like fabric, was ingeniously repurposed as some kind of avenger's weapon.

Bare-breasted, she sprang upon the father, who had lost his balance along with the table's support. Yanking the flimsy remnant of her blouse taut enough to show her brazen knuckles, no less hard than the inciting nipple had appeared through it only a moment ago, she stepped quickly behind the enraged father and swaddled his head entirely, cinching the wattled neck no less murderously than if she were wielding a garrote.

The poor man looked like his head was bagged for the gallows, and he could hardly have failed to notice the pinch of the noose beneath his chin. But Sigrid's sole intention was to corral him back to the saddle leather of the couch from which his son had bucked him.

When the man was at last settled, as dazed as a blindfolded child turned too many times at a birthday party, Sigrid unveiled his chagrined and blushing countenance with a magician's flourish, the flimsy tunic unfurling from one grandiloquently raised hand. The entire clientele of the bar and the restaurant leapt to applaud.

And the boy?

Perching herself nimbly on a barstool, Sigrid took him to her breast no less naturally than the enthroned virgin suckling her unnatural birth in paintings meant to bring devout pilgrims to their knees.

**

The title of Sigrid's notorious book, *Against Play, A Guide for Parents*, came to mind when I considered the fact that the flagrantly bared chest of this child psychologist – into whose care children were now seldom placed – had revealed her to be an avid player. Shorn of any modesty, brazenly offering her offended nipple to the untamed child, had she not portrayed – even worse, improvised – the role of an Amazon-cum-Madonna? Her all-too-versatile role play now shook my confidence as to her real character. How could I trust her to speak her lines with plausible authenticity when she spoke to me?

Now she professed to speak openly of her estranged husband's – my dear friend's – *liaison dangereuse* with my leading lady who Sigrid had good-naturedly, or so I was pleased to think, baptized *the murder muse*.

Sigrid wished to tell me everything Dr Todorow had divulged to her in that chamber of confidence that married people, however separated they may be from that blessed state, preserve as a ruined shrine to their lost faith.

But could she put her trust in me? Was Siri not my chosen confidant as much as my licentious protagonist?

Sigrid seemed to be sucking on Siri's name like a tart lozenge that might be slipped from her lip to mine if the signals between us were right. Abruptly, she turned her platinum head so that the flare of the floor lamp, shining off the arm of the divan, spangled my gaze. She agitatedly shifted her posture in a bentwood cane chair with her bare legs crossed and her stiletto heels parrying against one another. The decision to tell all or keep me in suspense seemed to await the outcome of that duel.

She was looking away from me. But I could still follow the nervous wavelets eddying along her ruminant jawline. The lozenge was melting. But it hadn't melted completely away.

"You have news from the surgery?" My voice channeled the quaver of the anxious relative who paces the floor of the hospital waiting room that has been polished to the most treacherous luster for a leather sole.

I was waiting for Sigrid to crunch down on the slippery and by now translucent body of the lozenge before it dissolved on her recalcitrant tongue. Or had she already swallowed it?

"You must know that what I tell you happened in the way I am telling it. Unquestionably. Least of all are the illegalities and infractions of medical ethics. I am more distressed by the doctor's violations of simple credulity.

"All of this because Siri, the devious lover, had devoutly wished to *be* what she had only performed in the rainbow iridescence of her weightless soap bubble: a life saver.

"Fingers foraging in the patient's sloshing breast pocket for the elusive corpuscle of malignity, or cradling the corpulent heart muscle itself, thumping like a massive toad against the restraint of a closed hand. For the privilege of experiencing such sensations, Siri persuaded my husband to be her tutelary spirit, enabling her to search the human body for its most elusive secrets. She would do the exploratory poking for herself, under his guiding hand. She wished to be the skin on the bones of my husband's hands. You will recall Nurse Fever hovering translucently in Dr Solfried's surgical ectoplasm for five successful seasons. Could Dr Todorow not pull off the same special effect?

"But," she protested, "*she*, Siri, was to be the searcher. Her character was only the muse.

"Imagine the susceptibility of my poor Todorow's hubris upon being presented with Siri's impossible wish to put her fingers where her thoughts had been from the moment she'd been informed of her husband's fatal reversal of fortune. Pulmonary thrombosis. Well, she considered, if a clot had been thrown, surely one would be able to grasp the hand that threw it. If one could get a grip, how difficult could it be to break the arc of fate? Would she not, in that way, be able to bring her Solfried back from the dead, as indeed he had first come to her in the television studio?

"What she implored of the miracle-working Dr Todorow was commensurate with the miracles of her own vocation, with which she had so successfully flattered his imagination. One can be what one does. One could act and act upon. Could the gifted surgeon not find a way to let her do what his hands might guide her to be? Yes, you can imagine the susceptibility of my poor Todorow's hubris. Irresistible.

"The doctor considered Siri's proposition in the way one prepares one's most flattering face in the mirror.

"The rest of the story, I confess, defies comprehension, though each word of his telling it carried a living breath as evidence of its truth. True to life.

"The saved life? – it was not to be."

There was a pause, a fretting, a twisting of hands as though they were wringing out a sopping wet towel.

And apparently the doctor's wife felt the need to stand in order to carry the burden of her tale further. She stepped out of her heels, to gain a better footing. The padding of her naked feet on the cork floor of my apartment expressed the body's vulnerability better than the wringing of hands. Those she kept flat to her sides, as disciplined as a soldier on parade.

"Now, as it happened, there was another boy awaiting his fate. In the surgery. On the operating table. If Todorow's report is to be believed, this boy was the same age, and so he was plausibly sprouting the same wisp of pubic hair on his upper lips as *our* boy. For these events transpired at the very hour when you, Pan, were delivering yourself to the investors and our boy made his fateful lunge across the cocktail table.

"Todorow explained himself to the assembled retinue of his surgical team, rubber-gloved hands raised at their sides like firearms. They were a posse avid for the righteous adventure before the silver bullet surgery doors were set to swing.

"Were they surprised when Todorow declared that he would perform the surgery at a distance? A telesurgical pod had been prepped on the floor above. It was fully wired up and ready to be operated.

"Todorow must have sensed his team's mounting agitation. This was not standard protocol for such a procedure. With the bluff confidence of a painter commissioned to realize a princely claim of dominion over a vast land, he assured his team that the remoteness of the telesurgical pod would give him the widest view of what they all knew to be a perilously narrow body cavity. He meant to inspire confidence. He would direct the team under the craning, swooping, endlessly snooping surgical lights of OR #4. He would, from the ergonomically optimized console, be shoulder to shoulder with them as always, flexing the robotic muscle of Da Vinci's supremely antiseptic stainless-steel mandibles as he raised and lowered them soundlessly over the patient's open wound. An inelimiinable whirring sound would be all that broke the otherwise concentrated silence of the team at their monitors or focusing their microscopical magnifying lenses into the depths of the incision.

"Todorow had his reasons for reserving the telesurgical pod on the floor directly above the polished tiles of OR #4. But they were as remote as the surgical pod itself and from the life that was meant to be saved. Here I must tell you that my husband implored my credulity as a psychologist. He said he had his reasons for straying so far from the strict protocols of his profession. Could I not conceive of them as therapeutic?

"'Therapeutic for whom?' I had to ask.

"'Siri,' he intoned with an incantatory quaver in his voice, 'in pursuit of knowledge.' The conundrum of Solfried's death had blossomed for her into a fit of madness. The hermetic seal of bodily existence fashions such episodes of lunacy for anyone who queries the mystery of the dying breath. He went on: 'Once one sets foot on the circuitous path of such pathos, one is walking forever.'

"But I must not become distracted from the boy. He is anesthetized on the surgical table. The boy, pale of skin – perhaps you saw the obituary photographs – had been born with a surfeit of freckles, sprinkled across his nose and cheeks like cookie crumbs, also with the lack of a certain striated muscle in the wall of one ventricle that might have given his pulse the proper pace. Instead, his heart raced to ultimate exhaustion.

"The newspaper report lamented the maudlin irony of the child's prosthetic porcelain blue eye, the result of an all-too-pointed encounter with a sharp stick. The porcelain eye was a perfect match for the color that suffused the child's otherwise pasty pallor whenever fits of breathlessness convulsed his delicate, loose-jointed frame, conjuring up a spectacle of malicious puppetry. Have I said enough? Yes, I chatter too. Who doesn't want to add something more to reality?

"Most of what I've said so far can be read in the news.

"But only Siri's understudy would know that what I tell you now is true:

"Since the perfectly plotted reversal of Steiger Solfried's fate by a wayward vascular hiccup, Siri had besieged the doctor with a litany of questions. She murmured them into his ear with the pathological urgency of cardiac fibrillations. He bowed his head to her entreaties with nigh priestly solicitousness. These are, after all, questions usually reserved for the diadem of dimly lit windows mounted high in a church cupola.

"I imagine, dear Pan, that you can hear the prayerful mourner yourself, though the cupola is not your haunt. Again, if the doctor is to be believed, the catechism of Siri's grief was incessant:

"'What would have saved him?'

"'Tell me where the breath flies?'

"'Could he have held the breath and lived?'

"'By what logic does the body change its mind?'

"'How is death really pronounced? With what expulsion of breath?'

"'Is it certain there isn't a barely perceptible beat in an unfathomed depth of the bloodstream?'

"'Are there cells still imploring him to awaken?'

"'How – how can you be sure?'

"Finally, breathing questions into his ear was not

enough. Siri must palpate the body's answers with her own hands. She wished the doctor to share the sensation of holding the pulse on a taut line – like a fish, she imagined.

"'Take me fishing. I want to feel the bite.'

"Ordinarily, before acceding to such a request, Dr Todorow would have looked at the boy, anaesthetized on the surgical table, with as hard a stare as gleamed in the boy's porcelain eye. But this time, I tell you, it was Todorow's own false eye that tendered a vision of what was foreseeable. Todorow's judgment was blind enough to make him take Siri's hand and lead her towards the incandescent glow of the telesurgical pod that floated like a suspenseful thought above the iron-gridded ceiling of OR #4.

"The surgical lighting hanging from the ceiling grid in OR #4 sharpened the edges of the room with crystalline clarity. The surgeon socketing his eye to the telescopic wand that was the focal point of the pod was confident of his mastery over the distance from there to the patient's throbbing pulse.

"I trust your talent for suspense, my dear Pan. So I know you can imagine what comes next.

"The only communication between the OR and the telesurgical pod was through filaments of wire that traveled from Todorow's ear to a microphone, the mouthpiece of which was budded at the terminus of a flimsy plastic arm that sprouted from an aluminum headclamp. Think of how the mouthpiece quivered with his every breath.

"The scene is now set for you, dear Pan. You must already know what action will ensue.

"See Siri clambering into the surgical pod and hovering as close as body heat to Dr Todorow's lime-green scrubs. See her snuggling into Todorow's lap, her body canted slightly forward, like a downhill skier, towards the telesurgical instrument panel. Her hands, gloved in his, tentatively fingering the burl-knobbed robotic joysticks of the navigational console as though she were an emanation of Todorow's practiced dexterity. She must have caught her reflection in the yet unilluminated television monitor mounted in the center of the console. From just such a dark screen, and at the flick of a switch, Siri's celebrity had shimmered into your view, my ogling Pan, the first time you watched her playing Nurse Fever.

"So it should pain you to watch with me now.

"If the blinking illumination of the screen, when it awoke, touched a nerve in the meat of Todorow's already taut musculature, Siri would have been the conductor of that electricity. The circuit between Todorow and Siri was closed. As wrong as Todorow knew he was in his action, she only felt the rightness of readying herself for the mission that lay ahead.

"Although bereft of her own sensations, her fingertips, wrapped in his, were full of confidence in their fine motor adjustment to the swivel of the steel joysticks that were synchronized, I'm sure, with the dilation of Todorow's pupils as he torqued the focus of his concentration.

"You must now consider the boy on the table, dear Pan. The one with the scarlet gash in his chest. Pale, porcelain-eyed, thin-lipped boy ... the lips now twisted around the plastic intubation tube like stretched elastic bands. A chestnut lick of his hair sticks out from under the stretchy rim of the green paper cap that an attentive nurse has slipped over his brow. Beneath the pink eye-lids, scenes are set for him to dream upon in opiate-lul-labied oblivion. Until, that is, he becomes the dream, the dream from which his red-eyed parents will never fully awaken.

"Give me your hand now. What we are settled in to watch should make you shudder, as if we were two terri-fied children in an unlit room, peering slit-eyed at the flickering screen from beneath the bedclothes.

"The doctor tilted the screen to suit Siri's line of sight, pitched slightly beneath his own, and they snuggled together in what was now the fully operational cockpit of the telesurgical pod.

"A purring sound emanated from the console. Siri attuned herself to it. She recognized its similarity to the bell that rings on the soundstage, snapping the actors, fitted snugly into their respective parts, to attention.

"Siri couldn't have been taken more by surprise to learn that the livid wound stretched across the LED monitor, clamped at each end in the shape of a skinned almond, pierced by leaking tear ducts at its antipodes, was staring her in the face. Not a mouth: an eye. This *look*, Dr Todorow had promised, might be the answer to her questions.

"Todorow, facile to a fault in this exercise of gross professional misconduct, urged her closer.

"He is my husband. Your friend. Siri's adulterer. Our *fiend!*

"Todorow meticulously chaperoned Siri's bloodless

fingers around the burled stainless-steel knob, bringing a shimmering scalpel blade into view within the frame of the screen. What else would Siri have thought in her robotic capacity? She was no better than a flexing of the surgical muscle, becoming ever more granulated with each micrometric adjustment of the marionette's digits to the pulsing confines of the incision. Did she wish to shake off the guiding hand, if only to feel the brief panic of her own flesh feeling for itself? As they hunched together over the monitor with such cramped intensity that a mystifying fog momentarily breathed over the screen, I imagined Todorow chafing against her coccyx.

"Todorow penetrated the mystery for her by shaving the atrial wall with a barber's cool precision.

"So smartly did the surgeon ratchet the steel blade away from the consummated cut that Siri mistook his muscular aplomb for her own uncontrollable momentum. She involuntarily rotated the blade back to the deftly flayed flesh, thereby opening an unsutureable tear in the wall.

"'Try to reweave, between frantic thumb and forefinger, the disintegrating fabric of the paper tissue into which you have just cleared your nostril of a snotty gout. The mucus turns your effort to the slipperiness felt by a toppling skater blinded by the treacherous sheen of the ice.' What else could Todorow say in his defense?

"The masks of grief, foisted so violently upon the parents when news of their boy's tragic death arrived by messenger from a distant floor of the hospital, reverberated with howls better sequestered behind closed doors.

"Todorow, appearing in his conspicuously bloodless

robe, wanted to whisper to them of the fates and oracles known to his priestly order, from whom cause, perhaps even justice, could one day be divined. He urged their patience with explanations. He stood before them, palms up in a benedictory pose.

"The parents were, of course, inconsolable. Their eyes blackened with rage. The blood shrieked in their veins, coloring their necks. They tore at their scalps. They fell to their knees and pounded the floor until their knuckles turned purple.

"I wonder, Pan, whether you are moved by these bruised and streaming faces? Would you, for a moment, abandon your anti-cathartic bigotry, your suspicion of empathy, your contempt for the weak indulgence of strong feeling? Do you still insist on keeping the heart at a distance? I speak of your notorious refusal to be the good doctor in your art.

"Well, the licensed medical practitioner, however egregious his doctoring might have been in this instance, was no match for your rigorous emotional detachment.

"When the dead child's parents were escorted off-stage, into an elevator, Todorow wept, actually wept.

"I wonder ... Did water from the same well overflow in Siri's widening, whitening eyes?"

REHEARSAL DIARY
August 10
Scene 2: Bathroom/Razor Slash

So here we were at the scene in which our first dramaturg had, in concussive reality, taken a crippling fall off the edge of the stage when he was meant instead to be slashed with Savannah's straight razor. This time the more pragmatic dramaturg scooted his chair well away from the footlighted precipice, a bit too close to the bathtub for Vidallia's modesty. I whispered to her that a stick in water is never seen straight. Her body blush was not diminished by that truth.

When the time came, I stepped out from behind the mirror, right on cue, and, brandishing my own nudity as shameless as steel with a good shine on it, I raised my arm in readiness for the bloody deed. With candor in my stride, feeling the bounce of my breasts, the slivering of light between my legs, and imagining the eyes of the audience like a dash of cold water on my face, I stretched higher to make them imagine the cut would go that much deeper.

But my razor-edged grip, cocked for the deadly business at hand, went off prematurely. The ivory-handled blade – real for the sake of realism – slipped from my fingers and found deft purchase in the ample meat of Vidallia's canted thigh, as though I were an out of practice carnival knife-thrower.

I missed the femoral artery. But the ambulance was already screaming towards us.

I only just recall that it had been Siri's disingenuously generous notion to permit Sigrid Todorow to understudy her parts. The killers all.

"Let her play," she said. "We'll see how she enjoys herself."

Siri and I discussed the matter under the rent fabric of an abruptly clearing sky. Blazing sunlight lapped up the shadows of the tombstones littered around us like honorific specters of Dr Solfried's early career with Gretchen Fever in the bowels of Grant Park Memorial Hospital. The vanishing spooks spookily reappeared as vast, sooty smears across the afternoon's blue dome.

Under the shining sun, Siri's sequined black leotard appeared more deliberately artful to me than it did to the other mourners, who, shrouded in conventional funeral attire, and judging from the look on their wrinkling faces, found it merely contemptible. They rankled at the shameless upstaging.

But surely the grieving widow is entitled to her theatrics. I said something to that effect.

Who had known that Siri and Steiger Solfried had secretly wed years earlier, when their soap opera characters pledged their love for a vampire's eternity. The episode aired as a wedding special. Fans were invited to bid for invitations by phone. The ceremony was officiated over on set by a Zwingliite minister, in deference to Dr Solfried's family origins, going back to ardent Swiss defenders of infant baptism in the 16th century. The minister was clad in the stiff blue uniform of a Union Army general. He served two masters. His face was almost completely obscured by fastidiously teased mutton-chop sideburns and a well-greased handlebar moustache that curled into tighter and tighter circles like a hypnotist's spiral wheel. Unbeknownst to all who watched in the studio and at home, their vows were legal latches. The loving couple had actually registered under the law of New York State. Their vows belonged to a differently costumed reality, invisible to their swooning viewers. Perhaps that's why the actors clamped down on the words with as much force as the fangs they appeared to sink into each other's neck.

There was no such *double entendre* to Solfried's brass-handled, black-lacquered coffin, though it reeked of the prop room. It bore a golden crest: two fornicating goats wearing fiendish masks, gazes twisted over their shoulders like helpless dogs post-coitus, to witness the long-legged devil astride their backs. That devil, himself two-faced, returned their four eyes in his fiery glare thanks to the cut of outlandishly large sapphires inlaid in the protruding trompe l'oeil sockets.

As two red-faced and doubtless alcohol-breathing cemetery caretakers girded the casket with ropes they'd use to lower it into the ground, a gust of wind drew a curtain across the sun and a belligerent downpour commenced. It precipitated no less menacing a scene change than an actor's falling off the stage on the cusp of sitting down for tea. One step outside the template of blocked action and, like any mountain climber missing his ledge, the actor senses that the world has moved on from the play.

The wind moving briskly through the crowd seemed to have blown the features of an altogether different person onto Siri's face. The widow's grieving eye sockets pooled with tears. She lifted her cheeks to show them streaming. Mocking the weather? The decidedly out of character smile on her face was inscrutable. There was also an odd adjustment to her posture where she stood face to face with the suspended casket, as if she were staring down a ghost.

Or she harbored the ghost in her physique. An invisible wrestler had seemingly taken hold of Siri, under her arms, and was heaving her up and down on his back. The tremors in Siri's upper body nearly lifted her off her feet, planted as perilously as they were on the slippery rim of the freshly dug grave. The muddy lip that was curled back upon the lawn at the site of incision was as grey as the heart-shaped spade that stood nearby, where a mortuary hand had left off trimming the edges of the grave. The wooden handle stood as stiffly as any of the mourners beside the deep and waiting darkness.

The tightly assembled mourners – a mix of Solfried's cast and crew, and my own – shivered in unison behind Siri: a phalanx of inconsolable grief, solemnly awaiting the lowering of the casket.

Everyone was, I'm sure, as surprised as I was when the huddled mourners were driven apart by the dozen or so stolid steps that Siri took backwards. This she did at the precise moment that the casket began its descent.

I observed it all as if in slow motion, as the most disciplined directorial eye must. Siri's knees, the higher she raised them, seemed to pump air into her calves. The black leotard was stretching with every backward step. Like a vocalist building up a store of breath to launch a soaring aria, Siri snapped her head back. She seemed merely to yawn, though it was a howl in my ears. Her body, like a notched arrow snug in the tautened bow string, appeared to be trembling with tension.

Then Siri was sprung. Flying through the passageway she had cleared by her purposeful steps away from the grave, she now pitched forward towards the grave's edge. Her palms sank into the saddle of mud. Their imprints were revealed in all their ghostliness as we watched her snap her tailbone into the air, kick her feet over her head, untuck the full length of herself between her legs, and land in perfect gymnastic form upon the casket's unyielding but treacherously slippery lid. The casket crashed to the foot of the excavation and the pallbearers shrieked in accompaniment as the rope burned across their palms. Remarkably, the gymnast maintained her balance. Her arms raised above her head as if pulled by an invisible thread of aplomb, also pled for a hand up. The plush crimson ropes that had burnt the pallbearers' hands coiled around the casket in the bottom of the grave.

Siri was raised from the place of internment, lifted off the lid of Solfried's casket, the vision of an ascending angel or perhaps an escaping demon. The grip of the pallbearers on this all-too-lively body showed in their faces. As lines of incredulity at what had transpired in their midst drew the skin taut across their cheeks and foreheads, they hauled the harrowed widow to the surface of the earth. Siri's black leotard had lost its gleam in the deepening gloom of an unrelenting tempest. But her smile was intact.

Only when she was settled upon the ground again

could we see that one of her muddied black satin ballet-slippers was corkscrewed in the wrong direction from her body. She was grinning but leaning upon the ankle that the foot had disavowed.

***

And so it was that, in the hearse-like patient compartment of an ambulance darting through Manhattan traffic as recklessly as a woman doing gymnastics on the lid of a coffin, Siri reprised her unexpected proposal.

Sigrid's wish to be an understudy, Siri's understudy, should be granted. Wouldn't Siri be on crutches for the foreseeable future? It was all perfectly logical under the present circumstance. Siri was, of course, viewing things through a haze of pain-killing intravenous medication.

Despite the drunken sway in her voice, I nevertheless heard the argument she constructed as though it were being dictated with weary lucidity by the prescribing emergency-room physician who would surely be on hand for the discharge scene – once Siri had been moved to a surgical table of her own, that is, and her ankle set in plaster.

The set. It would become a more interesting set for the underground rumbling of the understudy, Siri promised. "It will rumble like the engine of your precious subway scene.

"Sigrid's actor will be different. We are opposites. Perhaps this tickles your taste for merciless conflict. You will see how she tries to play me playing. But I have already fashioned the role to be as unplayful as our ingénue understudy can imagine.

"Sigrid thinks the actor is only really the actor when the playing of the part is not apparent, when the disguise is all there is. She would make the effortful illusion the reality. Every gesture is to be taken for what it is. Every word sounds its sense as immediately as the odor of a rose.

"She, like most people, wants nothing more than to play the part with the utmost seriousness.

"I, on the other hand, am a fool for play. My performance is always a real performance, something happening beyond the stolid meat of the physical gesture, the all-too-apparent thing itself. My performance is always undisguising itself, however plastered with carnival paint my face may be. I would make the effortful illusion sweat its reality. I am sweating now. You will have to wipe your hands of me. Perhaps my ankle is twisting my words. These pain killers are the murderers of plain good sense.

"So, I say, let her play it her way. Let's see how she enjoys herself." These were Siri's last words as she slipped beneath a heavier blanket of sedation, her eyelids fluttering into the attending faces of the ambulance crew.

An erratically zigzagging moth, trapped with us in the iodine-fogged cabin of the screaming, lurching vehicle, flitted about my head until I could no longer resist swatting it with the hand that had, but a moment ago, rested comfortingly upon Siri's forehead.

REHEARSAL DIARY
August 16
White Box Scene/Bat Swing

Sigrid, my understudy, stepping where I was meant to step next, into a contourless pool of white light, peered at Hum who was still finding his mark, a white adhesive X shimmering almost invisibly on the white enameled floor.

Ho looked on distractedly, a few steps away.

Their white flannel outfits glared at one another in the storm of illumination that flared around them. The set was hotter than when we had first rehearsed the scene, I reflected, from my new, yet to be appreciated vantage. I am, for the foreseeable future of these rehearsals, a curious audience, set aside of the action, chair bound. Aluminum crutches are crossed at my feet.

Then a sound effect from the flies.

Before the actors were aware of the sizzle and the sparks raining down from the lighting grid, hung lower than usual over their heads today, a cloud of pitch-black smoke blew directly into Sigrid's upturned face. It turned her into the minstrel of the show. This was the wick effect of the white pancake that already masked her features. Her tongue leapt like a splash of blood from the violent coughing fit that contorted her mouth, making her unable to deliver the next line.

Sigrid doubled over and knelt upon a shard of the halogen bulb where the explosion had shrapneled it onto the stage floor. Real blood seeped from the rent in her white flannel trouser leg.

My good doctor peers intently at me – as he typically does over a mountain of glistening artichokes, a plate of tomato-glazed paccheri bristling with rosemary stubble, and the conspiratorially shared bloody steak still heaving from the grill-master's flame – before he utters a word. Typically, we refrain from talk while we are eating. He has been molding his thoughts like soft clay during the masticated silence of our habitual post-rehearsal dinner.

"Do you remember the wife with the knife?" I took the silence into my own mouth.

"They sat behind you. Then, that is. Your shoulder blocks the view now. Have you, by the by, taken to wearing shoulder pads ...? Surely you remember. You saved the husband at some cost to your normal gait."

Todorow's eyes brightened as though reflecting my words, but I failed to see myself in those abysmal mirrors.

He steered the conversation in quite a different direction. "How did you guess that it was a wife I wished to discuss with you tonight? Mine at that. Not the cutlery-wielding would-be murderess whom you wish to place in the way of what I know you know I must tell you. Let Sigrid be our muse for the moment. I have news of her understudying. I have it from our brawny lighting engineer who leaves his cigarette butts by the side entrance. The news comes directly from him, not you. I was obviously in the dark. Is that what made him brighten, like one of his own overheated bulbs, to tell me what he knew?"

Todorow accented the word "like" with a click of his tongue. Now the doctor was prescribing. "But let's start by telling each other *what is* rather than *what it's like*.

What do you say, my brother in cardiac aches? Can we not speak candidly of my wife, your lover, since these things are true?"

Furio, the waiter, interrupted this unappetizing bone of contention to remove the plates. His white cummerbund was besmirched with strawberry compote, a wound that needed to be bandaged. To make matters worse, uncharacteristically he interjected a commentary of his own.

"You are like brothers to me," he smiled. "No, not mine. Only sisters mine. But you are alike in your noses. Exactly the same. Roman. You must be Italian."

Todorow suddenly looked like a man about to sneeze violently. Furio briskly offered a napkin bearing traces of the strawberry compote that bled from his midriff.

Leaping from his chair, Todorow tore the offering from the aghast waiter's fingers and lashed it across his face with the force of a slap. Blood began to bubble from Furio's nose. The waiter staggered back a few steps into the path of the bustling maître d', who was ceremoniously unfurling his arm before a briskly paced party of two, as if leading them on a short leash to their reserved table. Furio, the maître d' and the lady of the couple fell to the floor in a tangled heap.

The man of the couple was now an involuntary bystander, a perplexed observer.

In effect, Todorow had unwittingly restaged the tableau of his own victimization at the hands of the knife-wielding wife who had set her husband on fire. Furio's face burned with the embarrassment of having to extricate his head from the maître d's lap. The boss himself was trying desperately to regain his aplomb under the burden of Furio, who was now struggling to rise from his hands and knees so that he might regain his feet and give the boss a helping hand. The woman, having reached out to an adjacent table to break her fall, had shrieked upon seeing the steak knife in her hand. She toppled to the floor, impaling the knife blade between Furio's splayed feet.

Todorow, dizzied by the melee, appeared to be all the more enraged that Furio's interruption of his prepared remarks had set in motion an even more distracting succession of noises and altercations than those he had planned himself.

I piped up with, "That's why ticket-holders are never admitted once the performance is underway. They can't hope to catch up with the twists and turns of the action."

Trying too hard to salvage my unacknowledged witticism, I cued myself to stand abruptly and address the couple's dumbstruck husband, who seemed rooted to the floor: "We are *in medias res*. Please make your way to your seat with the minimum of fuss."

Who else, at such a moment, could have smiled a silver lining into the billowing storm clouds of Todorow's irate visage? And smile he did, however grudgingly.

At once I saw that this *entr'acte* of a scuffle was my opening to pre-empt the speech that Dr Todorow had certainly over-prepared for the occasion. Furio had no doubt already shattered the mirror in which he saw himself carrying the speech off. As we know, rehearsals are accident prone.

"Yes, your wife. I must tell you that she is not entirely

yours. Which I think is what you meant to say, but with another meaning. That was before the interruption, the fracas from which these irrelevant people have just picked themselves up. No doubt they were as surprised to find themselves in such disarray as you would be were I unapologetically to confirm what a lighting engineer has rumored – that Sigrid is now Siri's understudy and has been for weeks. This in no way makes Siri yours by default, which I hazard was what you were thinking when you pried your mouth open in the first place."

These words could almost have been my last breath, I exhaled them with such frenzied force. Todorow refused to take up the challenge. He murmured something inaudible and lapped the oil from the empty bowl of artichokes, mimicking the inaudibility of his words with a strenuous undulation of his tongue. The bottom of the bowl gleamed, the very color of the artichokes themselves.

Only after a lazy pause did he dredge his more voluble self up from the bottom of that bowl, as if to show me that I had been talking to myself.

"Did you know that Siri's heart murmurs more loudly than her husband's did? How could you know? Such noises are imperceptible to a non-medical expert, a layman such as yourself. You are not the sensitive you think you are.

"I've listened. I've heard the murmuring. You should know that I hear the morbidity in her heart murmur, the way she feels it. Her worry is as easy to detect as her pulse. I am attuned to it. It's a tune you will never be able to accompany in the way I can. The heart murmur is, of course, a shy whisper of death. She whispered her fears back to me in a voice that pleaded for my care. She was that seductive, luring my surgical skills toward the heart of another under the guise of her own malady.

"She pretended that she was afraid for herself. Brazenly, she proposed to calm her fears in the bed that was no sickbed, my bed, where, in pursuit of 'the little death', her heart would match my own rhythmic thumpings. So much the better to bring out her defect for my expert medical inspection. So much the better to reveal my defective judgment.

"I admit: little did I suspect that, in listening to the murmuring of her heart, I would become the stethoscope of her own ruse.

"Yes, you could say Siri deceived me. She kept a secret husband whose heart was troubled with a clankier malady than the one she hears pulsing in her ear canals. If I could care for her – she accurately reasoned – my impeccable care for the husband might be ensured in all sincerity. One loves the loves of one's love – that's what she was banking on. When I promised to treat the husband, her trembling lip caught a tear of gratitude in which my doctoring demeanor sparkled magnificently before I lapped it up.

"And now I can see the pulse quickening in your suddenly roseate ears, dear Pan. Could you not imagine my willingness to be used? You think I had not measured her fever for Solfried by the mercury of my medical opinion, taken to its silvery heights? You forget that the doctor can heal himself."

Todorow's eyes narrowed as if to pinch my cheek. Playing at something avuncular, was he?

I batted that gesture away before he could conde-scend further. "You know what Siri cursed above her own pain as the emergency room doctor ferried her to a full ankle cast? Your *botched operation*, as she called it."

I wanted to dam up his words. But I could see that Todorow had prepared his speech in a manner that would permit it to flow unimpeded.

"Let me suggest that Siri is now on the opposite bank from you, my dear Pan. She has crossed over to me and burned the bridge behind her. I know what I know through my stethoscope. My ear tubes are, if I may be permitted to mix metaphors, clear-sighted. Her bosom trembles under the metallic chill of its finely tuned diaphragm. I offer her an ear tube that she might join me in counting the after-beat of each pulse. They are the shadow steps that follow her blood flow, even without application of the instrument. But it is murmuring a different message than the one you mean me to take from your lips now."

I tightened my grip on the stem of my wine glass, bringing it to my lips in quenching silence.

Then I spoke. "Perhaps those tremors of Siri's blood should be heard as footsteps padding *away from you* – since you were only ever side by side with Solfried when you thought you were by her side. Her husband's heart was the beat she followed most faithfully with those beautiful feet of hers, long and pale as delicate fish bel-lies laid out in the sun by the fisherman. Haven't you cast me as the fisherman in order to put me on that figu-rative bank opposite to Siri and yourself? Siri does pos-sess beautiful feet; however, we muddy them with our rhetoric. You killed her husband, whatever you say about the chance meddling of clotted blood. That is what I am saying."

"You can say nothing that will not persuade me of your malign jealousy. You forget, I am still married to a psychologist, though it is your psyche she cavorts with now. Of course, it takes no training in the psychic arts to surmise that you are a character like anyone else, whose symptoms are telltale enough for Sigrid to tally. Jealousy is just one of them. Why else would she be interested?

"As for my Siri – and I tell you, the clutching pronoun is well-earned – she is under my direction now. You were mistaken about Solfried. The husband Solfried was a disguise Siri wore. She didn't strip it off at the funeral. That was her putting it on. She herself expects and fears an early death. That is all she mourns for. She has placed herself in my care no less candidly than she might place my open hand upon the moist breath she exhales between her generously parting legs, and no less carefully than they once used to hold a mirror to the blue lips of the dying patient."

Only then did I notice that the doctor sported a cravat in the open crotch of his shirt. Who would not call the silken color mandarin? I told him, as nonchalantly as I could, that were it several shades darker it would look like an open wound.

"So, you think you are wounding me," Todorow said.

Under the pretense of balling his napkin, I saw him ball a fist. Were he to lunge at me, he would have to reach across the table, risking collision with the wine glass I had set down between us. Yet he struck the blow through the glass. The knuckle of his middle finger struck directly over my heart, which he had last touched with a merciful scalpel. The wine spatter added realism to the moment.

The impact brought back to me the sharpest memory of my surgery.

"Did you feel that?" he smiled. His black pupils sank to the bottom of the whites of his eyes.

"So now we are speaking of what is real. The wife I meant to speak of at this dinner was the one you meant to speak of as yours at last. As if you had taken her from me. Ordinarily I would cattily reply, 'Really?' But we agree. We are already talking exclusively of what is real. I know that you know Siri to be the nickname for Sigrid. 'Short for ...' they say in some circles. But it is the other way round for me. So, you will know what I mean when I say Sigrid is no more for me. Yes, you have created another character with whom I have no connection, except that she is foreshortened in my field of vision. Sigrid is merely the shadow Siri herself casts as the one being understudied. Know that for me, Sigrid, the shadow, is foreshortened to the point of invisibility. Nothing more to see."

***

Accidentally, I dredged my cuff through a greenish puddle of oil that Furio, in his haste to remove the plate of artichokes, had spilled between the doctor and myself. The light was pitched in a way that we were both reflected there. It was in the spirit of cleaning up such a mess that I now saw myself capable of clearing things up once and for all.

"You know Siri less than she might persuade you. I know you pride yourself on never having been a mere viewer. You never watched what we call *the television*, the vivacity of your medical screens notwithstanding. No. Never a watcher yourself, other than within the beeping confines of the telesurgical pod. But we are both acquainted with the technology, distinct from the physiology, as I'm sure you'll hasten to point out. I speak of pixels pulsing with the life of luminous bodies – for my ilk imaginary, for you so real. Now I want you to be patient, take a seat beside me, and share the program I am watching.

"Make a screen of your mind and you will know how to see into it. I will tender the images to you.

"First, see the nurse, Gretchen Fever. She is impeccably bleached in her radiantly starched uniform. She stands as erect as a ray of midday sunlight, dressing down a novice candy-striper in the disinfectant blaze of hospital corridor lighting. The meek striper, whom, if we saw her alone, would appear to be a nymphet rapaciously hunting for an eligible doctor, is already fairly stripped in her thigh-hiking skirt. Nurse Fever does not permit such flirting with the uniform: rolling the waistband down to raise the hem higher.

"'Healers don't whore!' is Siri's ludicrous line. But the attuned viewer can see that such badly penned officiousness, even more egregiously uttered, is an affront to the actress's obvious talent, restless in its chrysalis.

"Yes, during daylight hours Nurse Fever strides the corridors of Grant Park Memorial Hospital wearing the demeanor of Head Nurse as if it were a bronze and garishly feathered helmet of war. See her the way you never did, how you might have seen her if you had ever peered into that imaginary space framed in black bakelite.

"But do see. View her episodes. See Nurse Fever staunching a patient's spewing artery with an improvised tourniquet, snatched deftly from a silken recess of her white skirt. The skirt itself appears taut enough to rip when she sits astride the victim. They are trapped in a hospital elevator. The only other passenger clenches the ivory handle of a straight razor in his dripping fingers.

"See. Do see. See Nurse Fever, furiously astride the bedridden patient whose limbs are flailing, as if one could drown in the turbulent waves of hospital sheeting stirred up by such hysteria. Nurse Fever's open hand sounds like a wave crashing down on a flat volcanic rock when it reddens the puffy cheek of a morbidly obese adolescent.

"'I've told you before, dear, the needle tip is so sharp you'll feel nothing but the tiny sucking at an open pore, like the new baby who will soon be sipping at your nip.'

"You might even see Nurse Fever colorfully awash in the stained-glass illumination of the hospital chapel, resisting Reverend Handsome's supplicating embrace of her athletically toned legs. His hands, which would momentarily travel up the backs of her pearl-stockinged thighs, are curled around imaginary stumps in the empty space from which Nurse Fever has so swiftly removed herself. The fading click of her heels is the only answer to what must have been his ever-more-silent prayer. Because he is already kneeling on the marble floor of the chapel, he can barely totter after her.

"Now listen as closely as I have asked you to watch. You might even hear the jingly intimation of a red-ker-chiefed housewife flexing her fingers in a pair of blue rubber gloves above the ridged and gleaming rim of a toilet bowl.

"They usually manage to edit out the commercials from these circulating promotional reels. It is, of course, never surgically perfect.

"And yet you must see, see what I am saying. Having observed Nurse Fever in her blushing human incarnation by daylight, you must peel back your eyelids even more, to countenance the spectacle of her nocturnal avatar. See her as Dr Solfried's attendant bat, he marching, she flitting through the haunted tunnels that worm their ways underground, past dusk, and, as Nurse Fever's loyal viewers oh-so-feverishly anticipate, past the second commercial break.

"The episode's resumption is cued by a lugubrious blast of organ music. We are now in the haunts of the underworld. Buried under the foundation of today's gleaming Grant Park Memorial Hospital, President Lincoln's medical prison, as dark as the proverbially unquiet grave, is where Nurse Fever enacts the dream of her worst self. As the bat grips the perch from which it hangs, she cleaves to her alternate persona.

"But I do not psychologize, I merely wish to describe *The Horror Soap*.

"See Nurse Fever taking possession of Dr Solfried. His body is a blurry translucence. She steps right through him. Gowned and masked though he is, his ghostliness is entirely believable. She grips his scalpel hand as though he were wearing her like a glove. Apparently real, the scalpel shows a steely resistance to her fingers. Before she can make the first cut, the blade must pierce the ghostly hand of Dr Solfried. As she unsteadily guides the blade towards the patient, Nurse Fever seems to be scratching her way out of a gauzy cocoon.

"Let us not smirk and make sarcastic remarks about such rudimentary special effects.

"For a moment the double image of the hand – Nurse Fever's? Dr Solfried's? – shimmers. Then, like a bubble, it pops, yielding perfect focus to the incision that Nurse Fever draws, no less artfully than an initiatory pencil line on an immaculately white sheet of paper, across the throat of the youthful Confederate recruit who lies, already dead, upon the gurney before her.

"She leans into the parted lips of the wound for the ghastly kiss. The nourishment is still warm from the low boil of a life only just released from corporeality. See the rat tongues nibbling at the water's edge. The floodwaters lapping the tunnel walls would rot the doctors' feet, were they of this world.

"But see also Nurse Fever wildly rocking astride Dr Solfried's muscular ectoplasm that she, only she, can plump up with serviceable blood. Banshee shrieks and writhing torsos. Naked arms flying ecstatically overhead like kites snapped from their moorings. See the fangs. Yes, cringe at the sight of the lasciviously bared fangs.

"Well might we laugh off the tv antics for which you already manifest highbrow disdain. Think only that

Horror Soap, like any such residual lather, will wash with a simple wringing of one's hands.

"But now, having seen what you did not want to see, you cannot deny that our Siri – even the possessive pronoun can never quite embrace her – is more than one person.

"'Nevertheless,' you say.

"You do not *fall* for the gaudy trappings of my production? You won't be caught up in the machinations of my plot?

"You think you have already seen her two ways, active conniver and vulnerable patient, and you are persuaded by that steely double vision to imagine that what you see is still yours to see. You accept that, from the beginning, Solfried's wife (we all needed corrective lenses for that astigmatism) sought your hand solely for its ventricular caress. She sought your caress of her husband's damaged heart. She sought your expert surgical hand under the pretense of inviting you to pick up the pulse of our performance, to join our company as the new dramaturg. You would be the one to pronounce the production 'alive'. Dr Frankenstein would be flattered. But no, in this case you were actually *her* patient.

"Can you escape the feeling of coming alive as Siri's monster on the surgical table?

"So now her other face appears, soliciting your care for her own, diagnosed to be an uncontrollably tremulous heart. You imagine that she is all meekness under the metallic chill of your stethoscope. 'Mitral valve prolapse,' you explained. 'Imagine your lips blowing against the valve as though it were a red rubber balloon stretched out of shape. Imagine the prolapse like that. Enlargement of the organ is a risk. Leakage is inevitable. More perilous is the resultant backflow of blood. Such regurgitation can permanently halt the beat.'

"You tendered that ominous diagnosis. And so, you imagined that now she must run with your baton. I suggest you consider a rewrite. I can help you with a scene in which you find yourself fully in command of your powers, free of the debilitating delusion that they extend beyond the weakness of the body."

I waited. I saw the expression on Todorow's face freeze with the eternal serenity of carved marble. My empathy-laden peroration was met with the stunning silence of a brick to the back of the head.

The restaurant began to sway to some inaudible rhythm. I felt my chest adding a percussive alarm to this moment of disequilibrium. The tables around us were suddenly limber with movement, rendering my apprehension of our fellow diners a carousel blur of colors. I was the man on deck, struggling to find his sea legs in order to conquer ever-more-tumultuous waves of nausea – a word that I remembered even more sickeningly, contains the silent *sea* – drawing him into that involuntary tango which is danced between the outwardly robust body and its convulsive interior organs.

When I groped for a steadying grip, I realized that the dusky bags under Todorow's eyes, which usually gave the appearance of eyeliner washed with tears, now appeared luminous beneath the even-more-polished luster of his smiling eyes.

What unsteadied me most alarmingly was the metri-

cally rigorous pendulum swing of Todorow's long forefinger, perfect leverage for the scalpel, waving with
admonitory certainty across my narrowing field of
vision.

"Trust me, my fleet Pan, whether you like it or not the
baton has been passed."

REHEARSAL DIARY

August 25

Restaurant Cloakroom Scene/Butcher's Blade

Sigrid has *found* her Marvin. So she says. Turning the wig this way and that until the curls fall properly over her eyes. She wants to appear perilous on her golden-spiked high-heel shoes. She practices a tottering gait. Beneath the skirt she has even strapped on an enormous codpiece she purloined from wardrobe, the better to compete with the feminizing flounces.

These are Sigrid's *findings*, all too proudly displayed to the rest of the cast and crew.

As if the character is *ever* found. Finding the character requires no investigative élan. The character is here, already here, wherever the actor is present and active in space. I prefer the already to the ready. The character is diminished by the actor who is so self-deluded as to think of herself as a finder.

Well, the rehearsal resumes.

Navigating unsteadily in the direction of the crimson cloakroom curtains, Marvin, in studied haste, accidentally catches his hip on the corner of the absent attendant's collection counter. This collision causes him to drop the bloody knife, which is weighted most heavily at its point. It impales the sharply-pointed toe of one golden shoe. The blood that pumps like a geyser from the slit in the shoe belies the intended special effect. This gore was certainly not squeezed from a tube.

What Marvin had so lightly gripped was not the ready prop, it was the thing itself.

"*Where is the prop master?*" everyone cries out.

I had only just thrust open the crimson curtains marking the exit. Entering the auditorium through the exit during the rehearsal period is my superstitious way of warding off the fear of audience defections through these dimly lit escape tunnels on performance nights. Don't most of us read the exit sign as admonishing us to go?

Finding my way to the middle of the orchestra rows, and turning towards the stage, I was confronted with more menacing admonitory signs.

A roughly improvised jungle of papier-mâché trees and bushes, shaggy with leaves cut from rags, apparently painted with pea soup and bound together with plastic webbing, was standing like a withered bouquet in the center stage. A card scrawled with the inscrutable message "Park Scene" was set upon an easel propped against one of the proscenium walls.

Otherwise, silence. Emptiness.

I had, of course, seen this before: the stage set for a scene unauthorized by my script, abandoned like a relic meant for discovery by a keen-eyed archeologist.

A single spotlight cast dingy illumination on the scene.

As my gaze gradually adapted to the woozy chiaroscuro of the dimly lit stage, and as if I were painting the scene myself by sheer concentration, I noticed, like the hallucinatory feathering of an eyelash that can momentarily distort one's vision, a park bench. Another prop for my suspicion.

"Who's here?" My words sounded in unison with the echoing clap of the electric breaker-handle against its safety plate, bringing all creation to light, from house to flies.

I knew how to say *Let there be light!* and make it happen, even though those weren't the words I spoke. Lonely as Adam in his garden, I hoisted myself onto the apron of the stage and planted myself in front of the jungle of brittle papier-mâché greenery. From this vantage, I observed a riot of footprints all about me on the dusty floorboards.

No sooner had I contemplated their intricate tracery than the metal doors at the back of the stage, behind the last tier of black curtains, crashed open and an athletic thunder of footsteps rattled the stage. Feet to fit the footprints?

They surrounded me with such a swirling shuffle of rubber soles that they erased the footprints I had just been contemplating. They clamored round me, studiously oblivious to my presence. I now felt as invisible to them as they, in their frenetic activity, appeared faceless to me. They had gone to work on the task with amazing energy and enthusiasm.

In their efforts to free the jungle from its wire meshes, I could nevertheless see that between them they were shouldering the weight of a vaguely human dummy, faceless as a sock, arms akimbo, the shirt sleeves stuffed with newspaper. Only the lower body was convincingly fleshed, owing to the fact that the trousers had been yanked down to the ankles, revealing what appeared to be a department store mannequin's stiff rubber legs.

Was I invisible? Or were they phantoms of a dream from which I would momentarily be awakened by Todorow's cold hand, summoning me from the heat-soaked maelstrom of Siri's dressing-room couch, which, during her absence from rehearsals, I often treated as my own?

I stood upon the stage, abandoned, apparently undreaming, feeling more like someone dreamt of in the midst of the freshly unpacked stage property. Three or four bushes had been herded into a restive hedge before me. A low canopy of trees hovered over my head like a grizzled beard. I could even hear a sandy path scraping grainily underfoot. I stared at the dummy. It occupied the bench at the center of the park. The dark trousers it wore were pooled around its ankles. And now, like sewage bubbling up into my consciousness, came the recognition of where I was.

In the park. *My park!* Where I had been assaulted; a dummy myself.

I chided myself for not having immediately recognized it. Perhaps I might now find a park ranger to tender my complaint.

The image of the mime-detective, neatly fitted into his black leotard under the flapping wings of his trench coat, came more vividly to mind than my imaginary park ranger. Then I saw, as clearly as though I were peering through the mime's indispensable glass wall, Todorow's imposing figure interpose itself. I felt a constriction in my throat. I wished to put the question, "Why?" The images appeared to be superimposed one upon another, a cinematic effect alien to the theater.

Was it dreamt?

No. I was beginning to comprehend something unthought of until that moment.

The conspicuous traces of scenes never written for these rehearsals, like fake archeological artifacts strewn suspiciously close to the surface of things my excavating mind was already sifting through, were certainly meant to arouse my suspicion. The park scenery completed a thought, because it was indeed a scene of my own, true to life, but one I had not scripted. So many other scenes, unscripted by me and left for my irritable scrutiny when I arrived at the rehearsal hall every day, had been of lesser concern, until now.

The others were props left over from the abortive improvisations of another theatrical director renting the same space: a three legged table, a bottle, a glass, an overturned chair; the belly of a sailboat beached in front of a poorly painted sky with a starburst hole shot through the paper it hung upon; the sandy rural road upon which a papier-mâché dog lay in the hazy wake of a car that had perhaps been nothing more than a sound effect.

Or was someone interfering with my scenarios? Maliciously striking wrong notes? Spoiling the arpeggios of my fastidiously sequenced episodes, all of which are pitched to my rare canine frequency? I do not speak figuratively. I say this because I have a mutt's hyper-sensitive nose for the scent of an intrusive paw.

The scent that now assailed my nostrils, more potently than the spray of a treed skunk, was of rotting vegetation, squashed berry, and yes, of course, the mashed turd of the quivering hound, all mulching beneath the ragged branches of park shrubbery that rustled in my memory and now, on this rehearsal stage, bristled before my very eyes. Property of dubious provenance.

When I swiveled my gaze, there was no one to whom I could put my question. Only the empty mirror stared back at me where I lay on Siri's dressing-room couch.

Rehearsal Diary
August 30
Drawing Room Scene/Necksnap

Balustrade's bust is twice the size of Lawrence's chest. It might embarrass Sigrid's Balustrade to notice this, were she observing from stage right. There I remained as passive in my chair as my ankle in its plaster cast. Sigrid, fitted too tightly into Balustrade's livery, casts a menacing eye upon Lawrence. She takes her carefully counted predatory steps in his direction, as the unsuspecting young man, confidently attired in a jet tuxedo jacket and a fastidiously knotted tie, gazes upon the empty leather club chair, looking for his mark. Sigrid – I can see it in her face – is feeling lasciviously alive to the scene in which Lawrence will soon be dead by her own fair – or should that be foul? – hand.

Perhaps she is enjoying this too much: playing me while playing Balustrade. One might say of the understudy that she is *my* disguise in this run-through.

When Balustrade grips Lawrence's shoulder, guiding him to the tufted leather club chair, Lawrence improvises a playful pirouette for which nothing in the script is proper musical accompaniment. He has missed his mark, scanning the floor.

They are supposed to be gangsters, after all. But where is the iron gravity, the brutal manhood?

Balustrade reveals the massive hams of his hands, gloves the prop master has provided her with in the form of garishly pink latex prosthetics. How else would the breaking of Lawrence's neck be plausibly accomplished? As Balustrade struggles to recapture Lawrence's shoulders, which the latter's unexpected turn have danced out of reach, the effortful thrust of Balustrade's outstretched arm unbalances him. An awkward totter becomes an abruptly leaden fall. One of the gloves, fit for a prize fighter, has flopped at Lawrence's feet. Although Lawrence manages not to stumble over it, he continues his evasive pirouette, alighting upon a fringed throw rug, the set master's last-minute touch of decor. No doubt Lawrence's mark is hidden beneath it.

Sigrid, sprawled out in front of him, grabs a fistful of the rug upon which Lawrence is now stooping to extend a helpful hand. Lawrence's feet suddenly shoot out from under him. He lands on his back: sound of a piano lid crashing shut.

"Lummox," Sigrid spits.

What appears to be a crimson dye puddles on the rug's otherwise colorless fibers, where Lawrence's head has splashed.

My melodramatic skulking in the shadowy right aisle where it descended precipitously toward the stage – crouched as I was beside the last seat in row F, to be precise – would have befitted a character in one of the *Horror Soaps*. My eyes hovered just above the surface of shadow, where my attention to the activity onstage was bobbing upon the moment.

When I realized that in spying on the energetic bustle of the rehearsal company I was spying on myself, I should have let my head sink beneath the breathable surface of things.

The dummy's upper body was stuffed with crumpled newspaper that had been thrust into the barrel-chested torso and dangling arms of a gingham shirt buttoned up to the chin. But the crude handiwork of the costumier was most egregiously visible where the hem of the shirt was attached to the elastic waistband of a pair of flesh-tinted tights, stretched as they were over the hips and legs of a roughly dismembered department store mannequin. Large, looping stitches of yellow yarn bit into the heavy flesh of the tights mid-calf, to prevent the trousers from falling off altogether. The life-sized puppet was being handed around over the heads of five stagehands, their arms raised in the manner that typically accompanies victorious huzzahs in a sports stadium.

This might have been a mime show. Silence was concentrated in action.

Then the dummy was laid decorously upon the stage floor, beside the abandoned park bench, face down, its head buried in the low branches of ragged shrubbery. In the blink of an eye, the stage was as bare of human presence as the dummy's exposed backside, which rose moonishly above the waistband of the trousers. I moved more deeply into the shadow of row F, squinting over the arched back of the last seat in row E.

Actors appeared as mysteriously as the stagehands had disappeared. Unrecognizable to me, the two figures parted the already fraying bushes to find marked places on the stage floor. The faint creak of their movements pricked my ears.

A voice arising from the invisible well of one of the front row seats sounded a directorial cue. Suddenly the actors were tightening a knot over the akimbo limbs of the dummy. Then there was no telling one body from another. The violent act performed here was a disorienting echo of my theory of the *unwritten scene*. My pen point had never touched upon this squeamish memory. And now I felt the gingerly probing tip of the scalpel being readied to make a decisive cut.

I admit, I have versed my actors in the mysteries of the *unwritten scene*. It is the scene that is only enacted when the actors have reached the limit of knowing what they are doing, with faith that they are doing more than can be made plain by delivering the most rigorously memorized line of the author's script. More is meant than what one does according to the direction of the written scene. I have, somewhat embarrassingly, confessed that the *unwritten scene* is the sacred spirit of my thespian tribe. I further confess to indulging in directorial shamanizing that coaxes belief in the *unwritten* world out of which the author's words will nonetheless be spoken as written. But what actor worth his salt would be satisfied with the spent breath of a merely scripted utterance? He, she, must want to communicate that there is something more.

But this ... this was different. The scene I was witnessing honored no such sacred trust with the secret life of the author's words. This was not the talismanic *unwritten scene*. It was, brutally speaking, the *scene unwritten*. Certainly not a scene written by me.

So how could I be expected to know what would happen next?

Nonetheless, having witnessed this rehearsal from the depths of my spying shadow, crouched down beside the last seat in row F, only to realize that I might be spying on my dummy self, I suspected that I already knew what would happen next. It would happen thusly:

At the opening performance, I would be seated in the cushioned alcove reserved for the director, recessed in the only immovable wall onstage, tucked just behind the curtain and at the edge of the proscenium opening. I would be checking off scene #14, for example, and tapping the tip of my pen upon the subsequent numeral no less punctually than my finger on a doorbell. I might be sitting with one leg ramped over the knee of the other, idly see-sawing to the rhythm of my moving pen.

The engine hum of the pulleys would sound the reopening of the curtain for the new scene. I would, for the moment, rest my pen.

The parted curtain would reveal a jungle of park foliage. The scene would be played for the author who had not written it but who might remember it.

In the course of things, the dummy would be torn to

pieces. The two bacchants, man and woman, would return the audience's gaze with ravenous lips, dripping lipstick and face paint at its melting point.

Knowing that the conspiratorial eyes fastened upon me from some fold of dark curtaining backstage were anticipating a traumatic shudder of recognition on my part, I would simply play dumb. I would not show myself to be scandalized by the spectacle being played out before me, under the direction of a piratical dramaturg, with a leading lady whose loyalty to me might now be assumed to have been an act. I would merely look down at the list of numbered scenes, move my pen to the next one, and, perhaps tapping my foot idly against my stool, wait patiently for the curtain to close. The play would then resume as I had written it.

Though I know they will be watching me, I will not reveal, in gesture or word, that the brutal and unwelcome insertion of the unwritten scene into the thereby disfigured body of my script – you might well imagine it heaving with regret – was indeed the most violent act of all.

Turning again towards the empty mirror staring vacantly back at me where I lay on Siri's dressing-room couch, I had to wonder: what now?

Rehearsal Diary
September 13
OBGYN/Laundry Chute

They are preparing the "baby in the chute" scene. Moving it up. It is now "Scene 3". The earlier the better, Pan determined.

"Here we set up the emotional dictum: there are no limits to our stoicism for what you must stomach." He typically speaks as though the audience were present, eager to be instructed, as obedient as the actors who must hew to the mark of his directions.

In the scene, a middle-aged woman wears an overcoat and scarf, as written. She is bearing the infant from the mother's hospital room.

As Midge, Sigrid struggles to keep her footing due to the high sheen of the hospital corridor floor. She has not removed her onyx stockings. Her footsteps hurry beneath the hem of her coat. Behind her, further down the hall, the husband stands with hands in his trouser pockets. He is rocking on his heels and apparently speaking through the doorway of an open hospital room. The bundle cradled in Midge's arms is ridiculously inert. She doesn't even let her elbows jiggle loosely enough to hint at a rocking motion. Grandma with a grimace.

Now she is hastening towards her purpose. Her hand flails to catch hold of the stainless-steel handle of the laundry chute. One stockinged foot had shot out from under her on the icy sheen of the floor. Had she been on actual skates she could not have been sent off balance with greater momentum. Her forehead strikes the wall above the laundry chute. The impact is as loud as the crack in the ice at the instant the skater disappears. The bundle unravels at Sigrid's feet to reveal a brown, tufted jungle-monkey, a yellow smile as broad as a banana on its face; a toy pilfered, it seems, from the cradle of the prop master's still wailing infant daughter.

I call it *mutinous, treasonous*, risking the kind of bombast that would demolish the most ironclad performance of outrage an actor under my direction could muster. Those, nevertheless, were the words coming to a slow boil in my consciousness as I carried the pot forward to what I knew would be the hotter flame.

Siri and her now all-too-fallible doctor faced each other across the table that was usually served by Furio and reserved for myself and my dearest friend. I sensed they were stroking each other's thoughts in a concupiscent huddle. Blind to my entrance, red-faced with conspiratorial intent, they were oblivious to my savvy intuition about where they might be found between rehearsal sessions on a grey afternoon such as this.

La Bussa was almost empty. It was too late for lunch, too early for dinner. Only two tables, littered with breadcrusts and drained cappuccino cups, were occupied. Only one waiter, wax mustached, unknown to me, met my gaze from across the ruby-hued salon. He posed against the wall, making a diptych with the gilt-framed portrait of an ermined Florentine aristocrat. Neither of them could disguise a sinister smile.

Had I approached their table, revenger's weapon in hand – sabre, pistol, blunderbuss – they, by which I mean Siri and her doctor, would have reacted with no-less-melodramatic alarm, though they pulled what might have been burglar masks over their faces as they turned toward me, leaving only telltale eyes and mouths for me to read.

Abruptly, Siri rose from the table. Her armor shone in the leather of her short, heavily riveted, epauleted jacket and taut pants, all in black. Her costume recalled to me the spring of the acrobat who had appeared to burst from the clothing of her familiar self at Solfried's funeral. Only the white glare of the plaster cast, burdening her ankle, detracted from the stance and – another ricochet of memory – brought the mime-detective to mind. The pinkness of her exposed toes clashed with the black image of that rescuer.

Her hands on her hips were, like his, cocked with authority. In the park I had imagined the detective's palms itching to draw a firearm in my defense.

Saying nothing, Siri approached me with a briskness that made me think she could walk right through me as easily as through the ectoplasmic shroud of Solfried's character on the set of *The Fire in Nurse Fever*. The steps she had taken towards me caused me to freeze in my own. Her hands upon my shoulders were nothing less than the talons of some bird of prey.

Here was I, face to face with the queen of the *Horror Soaps*, from which black lagoon I'd so famously dredged her all those seasons ago.

I heard my cry of complaint hover between us on pitiful sparrow wings. The effect was as ludicrous as the dialogue sounded in those bleakly arid studios where the words of the tv characters fall through the dead air of the broadcast.

"I know you are something other than you pretend to be, *rapist!*"

Having uttered the word, I could not resist pressing the charge.

"Amateur performance is bad enough, but to purloin a scene of action is licentious!"

Here we were in what I realized was a familiar rehearsal

space in the abandoned hours of the afternoon, in a restaurant that would resume its well-heeled bustle in a matter of hours. Here we were free to play without a script.

So I pushed Siri aside, pulling the curtain on the figure of her collaborator, still seated at the table. Todorow's eyes had shot up in his head like cockroaches scurrying for cover under the white glare of a suddenly flipped light switch.

As he stood up, his mouth tore open, as if he had stepped on some dragging hem of himself. Wasn't he tripping over his words to say them? At least I hoped I had put him in such a panic.

"If licentiousness is your complaint, my dear Pan, consider the succession of scenes you know all too well that are all too perfect repetitions of themselves – killing after killing. Haven't you killed all surprise with all that killing? What you need is more playfulness. Much more. Let us purloin a scene or two for laughs. Let us restore your capacity for surprise. We are, though you may think otherwise, here for you."

That was Todorow's sole parry.

Being a tall man, his next move revealed, with exaggerated sprightly action, his acrobatic tutoring by Siri. He feigned a pratfall, landing flat on his back. His legs thrust straight into the air levered him onto his shoulders. With hands all-too-stolidly planted in the deep pile of the carpet, he relaxed into a neck roll and gave a snap to his spine sufficient to set him back on his feet. It was a formidable display of athleticism, a performance lacking only the mini geyser of sawdust that would have erupted in the center ring of a circus.

But what was the purpose of all this?

He had pushed himself away from the table and off the legs of his chair in a demonstration of lithe intent. I would have preferred that he had been propelled in that direction by the swiftly falling shadow of my appearance before him. Yes, I had aspired to have that melodramatic effect on him.

Preoccupied as I was with my own theatrics, I had missed another piece of their contrivance. Having thrust Siri in the opposite direction during my advance upon Todorow, I missed – until I felt a sharp tug at my trouser leg – her miming of a death scene at my feet. There she lay, a decorous corpse. A patina of shelf dust from the prop room flecked the length of her black leotard like dandruff. She presented as her own dummy. Was there a message in the obscure tautness of the spandex?

The thought that all this had been laboriously rehearsed – that I, the audience, would arrive in the manner just rehearsed – brought me to the boil. They had arrived at the theater before me. They had set the stage against me, stealing *my* scene, a scene I had blocked to very different effects.

***

Needless to say, I had meant for things to go otherwise.

In my version, they, Siri and the doctor, would have been sitting in the dining room of *La Bussa*. My minotaur existence would have been hidden for the moment in the labyrinthine longueurs of a cloudy, wet, late-afternoon lull in rehearsal. Such weather, especially at the end of a long day, fatigues us, making our every thought take a blind turn. One seeks the more comfortable posture of the would-be napper tucked up in bed, waiting for the restful moment that refuses to come. In this state, I would have surprised them as though they were unsuspecting lovers, the lovers in the motel scene perhaps.

But the ballistics of this scene would be different. Verbal projectiles only, targeted at each of them. Two short bursts from my articulate muzzle, with fatal accuracy.

I would shoot Todorow first. "The good dramaturg is indeed meant to be a good doctor, even if, in your case, the roles are reversed. And not unlike the good doctor, the good dramaturg never fails to remove the last sponge from the freshly sutured cavity. Nor does he self-indulgently imagine himself introducing the hairy palps of a rare albino arachnid into the wound."

Yes, I would remind Todorow of his licentiousness with the five-chambered heart of the *bee girl*, something he'd confided to me at a dinner in this very restaurant. That was when he vaunted the theatrics of the surgical theater, heedless of the real life tendered to him by the infant's almost hysterical parents.

"One down," I'd say calmly.

As Siri sprang to her feet, involuntarily hoisting her epauleted jacket high above the waistband of her hip-hugging sailor pants, I would point the gun's smoking muzzle at her bare midriff. Hampered by the heavy plaster cast on her ankle, she'd be unable to flee. Then, cranking my jaws open, I would summon words as hardened with reality as my gritted teeth. How could I resist an explosive dénouement?

"You imagine that you have commandeered my theory of the *unwritten scene*, since I have never spoken of my writhing nakedness in the brutal underbrush and fetid dark except to the mime-detective who appeared, so *deus ex machina*, in the wilderness of our park. Yes, *our* park. I take the liberty of sharing it with you now.

"And the detective? The mime-detective sticks in your memory, does he not? Like a pin."

Then, turning back to Todorow, dead or soon to be dead at my feet, I'd put a point on it:

"Prick!"

REHEARSAL DIARY
September 19
Motel Scene/Bleeding Wall

In rehearsal they are doing the scene in mime – the opening, at least.

Sigrid's silent approach to the disheveled bed is panic-stricken. She has a hungry eye on the cresting linen wavelets ahead of her, as if such minimal surf might be enough cover for her nude body when she moves to take her place under Claudius' curly black head. Her modesty is apparent. But her hesitation to stretch out on the bed protracts the length of time she is exposed to the, as she sees it, spellbound eyes of the crew.

She had bitterly protested this scene of "gratuitous nudity" to Pan. She had earlier confronted him in his official lair, squeezed between the flimsy back wall of the set and the brick wall of the Italian restaurant.

"Gratuitous violence, gratuitous nudity. Gratuitous violence is gratuitous nudity," Pan had scoffed, his voice loud enough to carry to the restaurant side, giving pause to a fork being lifted from plate to mouth. Those of us awaiting Sigrid's return to the set were already tuned to his words.

Claudius was waiting on the bed, staring impatiently at Sigrid's attempt to hide her nudity behind the halting motions of her body. He lifted his poodle curls, the better for Sigrid to slide the full white length of herself ever so discreetly beneath him. Still she paused, a reward to the voyeurs, though this was precisely what she wished to avoid. Perhaps it was her mind refusing to let go of her body. She is such a deep thinker about her role.

Though Sigrid made no sound, Pan's words must still have been booming in her ears, enough to cause the tremor through her chilly torso that sent her toppling towards the bed. As she lost her footing in her bid to outrun the embarrassment of her exposure, her ungainly height tipped her all the more forcefully off balance. Her bony brow struck Claudius's forehead like a mallet, rendering him unconscious.

Unconscious he most certainly was. Otherwise, wouldn't he have lifted a hand to staunch the crimson flow?

That a mime-detective was the only person who knew how the rank perfume of canine fecal underbrush and deliquescent rat rose in my nostrils like the two sticks doctors tweezer together in order to straighten a broken nose was, for me, a blessedly silent solace. He offered a supportive arm, gently levering my fragile frame into the back seat of the patrol car, where he saw that what I sought most of all was invisibility.

He was, of course, a real detective, not a mimer of the profession. Once he'd cinched what looked to me like an authentic trench coat over the more amateur *artiste's* leotard and settled into the seat beside me, taking his pen and notebook briskly and oh-so-professionally in hand, I understood how I might make something even of my victimhood.

The squad car engine was ticking over. It breathed warmth upon my exposed skin through vents purring at my knees. The interior light was mercifully turned off, that I might not inspect my dishevelment. The mime-detective held a flashlight the size of a fountain pen between his teeth and aimed it at the freshly exposed blank page of the notebook.

"Victoria and Victoire," he said, taking the flashlight from his mouth. "And you say your rescuers were also your attackers?" The question, thick with mucus, caused the mime detective to clear his throat, all expectation of the mime show gone in a gulp.

"How will we find them now? They are even more elusive if, as you claim, they are trained actors acting both parts. Attacker. Rescuer. Which was the act, which the action? If I am to help you, I need your help."

I giggled. I'm told those in fear for their lives are prone to do so out of a surfeit of adrenalin.

Then I blurted out something that a victim of crime would rarely have the confidence to say: "What better disguise for the crime than the solicitous embrace of the rescuer?" The clarity of this thought startled me. And before I knew what was what, the words formed in my mouth like stones athwart a furiously running stream: "I *know* those two.

"No, physical resemblance is not my criterion for identifying them. Nor a recognizable face, that banal nudity. Nor bulk or height. Not even the litheness of hips in their vaguely acrobatic leaps. Neither mug shots nor wanted posters would serve to identify them.

"Did they even have faces? Of course they had, but not to my eyes. It was the act they committed that had a face. Victoria and Victoire are only names. Still, as I have said, I *know* them. I can only describe the face of the deed they perpetrated against me – or my body, I should say. By deed alone I know them.

"Or let's say I know the kind of people whose faces are worn as masks for other people. Furthermore, it is entirely possible that the real plotters against my dignity employed proxies. The proxies would of course have been encouraged to make up fanciful names. Or, more improvisationally, they named themselves fancifully to better disguise themselves as doers of the deed, knowing how mystifying the scene would be rendered by that *coup de théâtre*. I suspect multiple duplicities. Disguise upon disguise is the métier of the actor who, especially when the act is most egregious, desires to elude recognition. Like the common criminal, no? And then there is the fact that they vanished as chimerically as they appear now in my recounting. Yes, the vile deed was so deviously plotted."

"To what end?" the detective dryly but indulgently enquired.

"*To what end?* My question and yours are not the same. I tell you, I *know* those two. Or four, if they were proxies. The multiples are perplexing for you, I'm sure. A bigger cast, a bigger mystery. Does it offend you that I am miming your detective ways? Well, I too am a plot solver. By vocation. So don't take offense."

The mime-detective bit down on another inch of the flashlight and redirected its searching beam at my face. He would have noted the composure gathering there. The power of deduction is such a restorative elixir to the flesh. I could feel the slack skin of the pitiable victim made taut again as I pieced together the skeleton of the crime.

"The leather portfolio, my script. Victoire absconded with it. To that end, perhaps."

REHEARSAL DIARY
September 21
Scene I/First Pistol Shot

Sigrid as Icon is finally flourishing the pistol. The manservant Gibbon has pointed his foxtail, nailed to a stick, further down the trail. Making way for his man, Gibbon takes three mincing steps towards the back of the set, a ridiculously dwarfed stand of paint-sprayed spruce trees. They are spring-loaded against a massive steel frame upon which they are meant to collapse for quick changes of scenery.

But in order to train his pistol on Gibbon, Icon has to take the tails of his black waistcoat in hand, no differently than a bride must lift her train on the dancefloor. As he swirls into position, one of the tails catches in the mechanism of the trees. The cocked spring releases with the resounding violence of a hundred-year-old sequoia felled in the forest. Icon leaps out of harm's way.

The manservant has, of course, stepped back from the barrel of the pistol and got too close to the forest. His arms, flung wide, become latticed with the lower boughs of the greenery. When the mechanism snaps and the stand of trees shuts upon its steel frame like the guillotine bar of a mousetrap, the actor is snatched backwards and into the air, heels flailing to find a solid footing, until he ends up flattened upon the forest as if the felled tree had fallen on him.

Sigrid's Icon, staring bleakly at the guillotined actor, lets the pistol clatter to the floor.

No one moved until the ambulance siren resounded in our shaken heads.

I sat paging through the dog-eared scenes of the script at my makeshift drawing table, sheltered between the paneled stage set wall and the brick wall of *La Bussa*. Deaf to the mating sounds of china and cutlery on the restaurant side, I was startled by kindred voices storming the paneled rampart of the stage set.

The flimsy set wall shivered. On the other side of the divider, the scene that was set was lit brilliantly from the fly grid above it. The lights began to sway violently, sufficient to throw the shadow of the set wall upon me like the seismic shudder of a collapsing house. An ape, having escaped from the nearby zoo, could have been swinging from the grid.

From the prop-cluttered wing, stage left, I entered upon a scene of tumult. It appeared Siri and Sigrid, in the midst of the rest of the cast, were struggling for the same floor space.

They were rehearsing the additional scene, only recently added. The written directions stipulated that in the wake of an explicitly non-fatal act of sexual violence a curiously costumed detective should appear sporting a black leotard exposed by the wind-blown flaps of his trench coat.

When my cast posed the obvious questions to my proposal – "Then who would be killed? Without a proper killing, what place would be proper for this scene in our play?" – I promised that the detective would be *properly* dispatched.

The intense light, still undulating over the tableau of actors and stagehands, shone with even greater lucidity when I looked up to see that someone had tossed a straw broom aloft, handle first. The broom swayed along with the entire lighting grid in which it had snagged.

"I was sweeping the park from the stage," was Siri's explanation.

Siri's by now somewhat dusky plaster cast sounded the vehemence of a jackboot while she paced the stage floor. And yet, to look at her, one might think she was offering lessons in an entirely different gait – limping.

Sigrid as Victoire briskly crossed the trajectory of my entrance, to interrupt Siri's irate hobble. The rivetted epaulets of his leather jacket made electric sparks fly under the still skittery beams of light shaking from the grid. Victoire raised a flat hand against Siri's chest like an officious traffic guard.

"It is written: 'The detective is wearing a leotard under his trench coat'. A black leotard. Haven't you read the revised pages? And yes, Victoria has already scampered off. Only *moi*, Victoire, remains at the scene." Packing the accent with male huskiness, Sigrid barked this out at Siri.

She made a violent gesture, sharpened with a switch-blade finger, jabbing it in the direction of the detective who had apparently donned an already-perforated black leotard. The gash in the fabric gaped wider with every breath he took.

"Is this a dispute about costuming?" I had to put the question.

The dramaturg threw a stony glance at me from the opposite wing, stage right, looking to see how I would adjudicate the case. I was the man defiantly holding his breath at the bottom of the pool, waiting.

The dramaturg stepped briskly into the scene but

measured his steps as carefully as someone crossing a swollen creek on slick, mossy stones. When he gained more solid footing, he placed a hand on Siri's shoulder. He might just as well have thrown a net over her, given her reaction. Her hands tore the air with furious gesticulations. Filaments of the shredded net appeared as wisps of blood on Todorow's cheek, where what I took to be her act of clawing protest had snagged reality.

I was becoming engrossed in the action. It was going precisely as I had hoped to plot it. I would watch and wait to see what they came up with. Would Siri betray her lover if he refused to take my bait? Would he side with her insistence that the leotard defied credulity? Which of their false pretexts would play most plausibly to the other? I had endowed the scene with improvisational *largesse*, sufficient for them to reveal the fullest extent of their guilty consciences.

Siri spoke. "Your spouse, my dear medicine man, is indulging too much literal-mindedness in the costuming. A real detective would never sport a black leotard."

The dramaturg, gingerly blotting his cheek, breathed a barely audible whisper across the intimate space that had heated up so quickly between them.

Siri perorated. "My dead husband, whose heart you knew after all, even when he was wearing his most whimsical writer's hat, would never have entertained a mime-detective, not to mention a rape, even in the silly gloom of Grant Memorial. Whose credulity could survive all this?" Siri blew the words in Todorow's direction with the sanctimony of someone throwing a veil over a tombstone.

With a shake of his head, Todorow resumed his function. "I am only standing in for the writer, the director, this afternoon. I am not the writer. I do not make things up. Today I am not even the dramaturg. I am the executioner of the script."

Had I inadvertently given the dramaturg license to expand his creative repertoire, to be faithful to my character whom he now professed to play with absolute fidelity? In acknowledging this, was I thereby forgiving him for the crime I was accusing him of by writing this additional scene in the first place? I am not prone to such acts of generosity.

Casting his eyes over this discordant little orchestra, the dramaturg took a step back, lifted his conductor's arm and signaled the company to pick up the beat. I could see in the flick of his wrist the uncompliant tension of the fingers and his uncertainty that the gesture would have the magic-wand effect he wished to conjure into being.

Did anyone look my way for direction? No. I appeared to be in a blind spot. Because I had written the scene, I suppose I was bound to appear outside the frame. Well, invisibility is the best omniscience.

In any case, the surgeon's fingers began to stir the air onstage as deftly as they might disentangle arteries in a congested wound, and the actors began to move along the path of the scene as it was written.

The script ordains a path through the park. I'd imagined that Siri and the doctor would feel the familiarity of their feet upon it, as they pulled the scene together. I could trace my own steps back to that path as perfunctorily as tucking in a dishevelment of my clothing.

But I had laid out the action more neatly. The path was the scene of the crime. The detective would be summoned to the scene by the perpetrator of the crime, better to disguise the violent act as an act of mercy. The ruse, once discovered by the detective, would invite another crime.

Victoire now stood to one side of his about-to-be victim, releasing the knife blade on its spring-loaded metal track from the sleeve of his leather jacket. With a snap of the killer's wrist, the knife was retractable. It would become invisible, should other policemen appear on the scene.

"Brilliant costuming," I said, finally entering into the frame. That was when Sigrid's blade pierced the detective's flank where the already rent leotard exposed tattooed flesh: a thorn-ensnared heart, beading blood at each prickly point.

The violent torsion of the detective's sprawling collapse upon the earthy floorboards had run the incision in the leotard all the way up to his armpit.

I attempted to muffle the satisfaction in my laughter by casting a hard look at Todorow, who appeared limp from his directorial ardor. Allowing my judgmental gaze to ricochet towards Siri, who now stood, broom in hand once more, at the brink of footlights, I sputtered, "So, what do you really think of that black leotard?"

"I think it reminds me of a stupid mime. You know, dumb."

***

What could Siri have meant? I felt snubbed by the awkward pirouette she made, swiveling on her weathered ankle-cast to resume sweeping the earthen stage. This amounted to little more than scattering the carefully laid path of dirt through the park beyond the circumference of the set and into the disgruntled laps of an audience that, of course, had yet to materialize. These were, after all, rehearsals. But what had the furious broom to do with that? The set was ready to be struck, in any case. Siri's head, slightly canted towards the floor, her shoulders swaying with each stroke of the broom, betrayed the profound self-absorption from which the gifted actor can dredge convincing characterization. For such an artist, even the most mechanical movements of the body can render a real person. She appeared to be exercising her craft and exercising it well.

But I would have expected she and the dramaturg, both wild-eyed, to have retreated by now into a feverish backstage huddle, panicking at the reveal of the black leotard. What should they do? Yes, what should they do? What indeed should they do?

So, was Siri acting? Was she acting in spite of her inexplicable enthusiasm for the idea of having Sigrid act in her place over the course of these rehearsals, at least until she, Siri, regained her stride?

It had been my patiently calculated intention to witness Siri's and Dr Todorow's involuntary display of red-faced conscience. Such is the pox-like flush with which the guilty are afflicted at the moment of their discovery. I wished the blood itself to act at my direction.

Or was their showy insouciance an attempted act of exculpation, acting their innocence?

Or was the act of swinging the broom, not to mention

the dramaturg's blithe inattentiveness to the dying mime-detective, nothing more than obliviousness? If so, one must presume they were not acting at all.

Or had they perhaps not acted at all in the park, where my memory tracks back to the declivity of filthy underbrush where a long dead rat is emulsifying still?

"Next," was all I could summon, signaling to the property crew with the flat-handed gestures of a policeman directing traffic. A change of scenery might, I thought, shore up the props of my reality, as superfluously paradoxical as that may seem.

REHEARSAL DIARY
September 30

It is time I wrote a scene of my own.

I am past rehearsing what is meant to come. The diary is an all-too-retrospective view of days. Worse still, it is an impediment to what is coming, no less so than my shackled hoof was an impediment to taking steps forward. A woman with a cast on her ankle impatiently awaits the moment of liberation, ignorant of where those footsteps will lead.

And a rehearsal diary? What good is a faithful account of events that defy rehearsal, susceptible as they are to perpetual accident? It is an affront to the pretense of practice. So from this moment I am dismissing the days I have put on record in these pages as a litany of unforeseeable accidents: cracked skulls, inadvertent knife wounds, near electrocutions, errant pistol shots, actors snatched into the snapping jaws of stage machinery. Now I am only interested in what is to come.

My doctor has taken a saw to the plaster.

So now *I* am what is coming. I am coming to give the opening performance. On the ceremoniously appointed night I will appear, a person in person. I look forward to the event, a ripe orange into which I have already dug my claws, ready to peel back the bitterness from the sweet, succulent flesh.

Need I say that I have dismissed my understudy from her stand-in duties? From now on she merely stands by. I have resumed my roles.

And yet, there is more to say.

****

We, the understudy and I, have quarreled about how to act.

I have already described the scene. Rushing to find her mark for one of her most sobering acts of violence in the play, Sigrid's unshod foot, blind to a long streak of slickness on the waxed linoleum, slid into an involuntarily pratfall.

At which I laughed from the sidelines. I put a point to the laughter, however, hoping she would feel me needling. "This is the rebuttal of your theory that the actor should play the part unto palpable reality, as if the performance could be a perfect fit for the costume.

"You, Sigrid, have a cannibal's appetite for character. And yes, of course, I have chosen the wrong word in saying you think the actor should *play* the part. It is well known that you come out against play, even in the realm of childhood, where you have labored though never birthed.

"You quibble that one works to play.

"Even the role of understudy you pursued to prove your point. You were the most diligent student of each of the many parts I am meant to slough off, with multiple costume changes, as I advance to ever-more-violent acts. The scene changes required in this merry-go-round tragedy fashioned by our fleet Pan oblige our audience to turn and turn again if they wish to follow the transmutations of the killer killing killers. Yes, turn and turn again. I think of the ratcheting wrist of a playful child, her firm grip rotating the metal body of a kaleidoscope.

My characters are the colored tesserae of a relentlessly metamorphizing mosaic.

"You, on the other hand, see and seize but one thing at a time. You find in each character a nature that you can manifest as itself, or feign the conviction that it is so. Your mind imagines itself capable of becoming what you are not. You wish to inhabit the appearance of something so alien to yourself that you might experience it as viscerally as the contractions of the womb ... and you a stranger to birth. Well, we've already said so. Do you feel the characters wriggling between your legs when, with strident steps, you take your mark onstage: the aristocrat at a hunting party, the thug with the garrote threaded between his fingers, the signora lashed to the rack, the blade-wielding daughter at her bath, the adulteress in the bed of her motel room when she is discovered by her husband, the faithful transvestite 'done wrong' in his lover's embrace, the mother disposing of her fourteen-year-old daughter's unwanted child, and, for you, the *nonpareil* others whom you faithfully make known to be other than yourself?

"But you are wrong," I said. "The proof is in your pratfall.

"You are where you lie on the slippery linoleum. And I mean it both ways, even if you can swiftly raise your body from its undignified sprawl, patting handclaps of dust from your elegantly trousered rear end. There, where you lay like the man with the banana peel mashed onto the heel of his shoe, you were acting, really acting, instead of burdening the act with a footlocker full of character traits.

"So the pratfall is what it means. It means what it is. You must know only that it happened so that you might resume the act unencumbered by the adipose pretentions of the actor, the sickly, pinkish obesity of the lie.

"Yes, the proof is in your pratfall.

"I can tell you that Nurse Fever, svelte as always she was, had been instructed in the dietary laws of acting without the actor. One does not need to put on that extra weight. You can't imagine how ardently Solfried, her vampire lover, coached her in the underground surgery that was her first *tiring house*. And don't lose sight of the irony. Our sponsors' jaunty musical interruptions of the episodes were operatic testimonials to miraculous feats of weight loss, the laundering of clothes that would need to be purchased to suit the new, slimmer body, soiled as it must become with the sweaty labor of reborn passions.

"So, was the actor in me reborn? I will tell you.

"There I was one day, attempting to nurse the character of the haunting succubus through a muddling scene of vampire romance. Nurse Fever's diaphanously clad body mocked the ectoplasmic flesh of the army doctors in the moldering corridors of that long-buried hospital. They were no more solid than smoke wafting from battlefields on which their patients had been wounded.

"But you must attend instead to Nurse Fever, struggling in the grip of my aspiring actress, struggling to suit her character.

"I remember flubbing the already bumbling line, 'Your deadness sparks the life in me' – begging the words to tell my actor's body how to sparkle.

"I couldn't have forced a more raucous guffaw out of

Steiger Solfried if my whole hand had tickled the under-side of his ribcage. The flubbed line had been my cue to descend upon his prostrate form, arousing the ghostly vampire from his coffin to begin his nocturnal rounds in the wards.

"Instead, the actor's hand went up in admonishment, halting the action, causing the camera operator to remove his eye from the lens.

"I must tell you now that his abruptly sober tutorial was the sought-after light that is supposed to sparkle in the best performance. He lifted his eyes to declare: 'Siri, be like an acrobat. Move in the air as if there were no physical obstructions. But not *as if*. Pretend nothing!'

"He closed his eyes and let the character's head fall back to the bottom of the coffin, which resounded like a knock on the door."

With the chalky heel of my ankle-cast I hammered the floor twice. I mean to echo my Solfried's tender admonition. Perhaps Sigrid could feel the truth of what I was saying in the resonant soles of her bare, slippery feet.

La Bussa will commemorate our late cameriere
Furio D'Agostino
at noon
August 29
Luncheon to follow

... read the announcement in my upturned palm as I shifted the umbrella from my more useful hand and with the tip of the umbrella opened the door to the dearly beloved restaurant. How could it any longer be the refuge – from the immediate downpour notwithstanding – that Dr Todorow and I had always taken here, at the sight of Furio's come-hither hand indulgently waving us to our usual table?

That's where, this afternoon, we regular patrons were meant to sit, and where Todorow was already stiffly rising from his seat. He appeared outrageously gowned and masked, as if for an imminent surgery. Upon seeing me enter, he raised a finger in the air. Had our encounter been taking place in his OR, he might have been summoning a sharp instrument to the cut. The ludicrous paper cap on his head, usually worn to protect the patient's wound against any loose follicles that might flake from the medic's scalp, seemed cocked with a jauntiness that struck a sour note.

Was Todorow's costume meant to demonstrate that he had come with all haste from the surgical theater? Had he not found a spare moment for a change of clothing, or was this costuming tailored to some theatrical antic that was brutally out of sync with the mournful event at which we were present? It was not beyond my imagination to do such a thing. Or, for that matter, his.

After all, we understood from the block-lettered newspaper obituary that the lifelong waiter, the last to finish his shift two nights prior, had exited the restaurant through a heavily armored metal door, as usual. That door secured the kitchen against an alleyway that ran alongside the building and emptied into busy streets on either end of the block, one of which was fronted by our theater. The alleyway was notorious for its shrouded and menacing forms, especially at such an early hour.

The authorities surmised that Furio had been mercilessly beaten no sooner had the door latch clicked shut behind him. No one was there to witness what happened; the other members of staff had exited hours before.

The killer had wielded a heavy lead pipe, the apparent discard of an emergency plumbing repair accomplished that night at a nearby eatery.

My seat, adjacent to Todorow's, wobbled beneath me. Todorow steadied me with a grip strong enough to stabilize a dangerously bobbing boat. Surgeon, sailor – the steering hand is the real vocation of each. And of the dramaturg, too.

Thunder clapped resoundingly, turning the attendant heads in the direction of the restaurant's rough-hewn entrance, the sturdy facsimile of a Tuscan barn door. We were safely penned in against the relentless rain and wind for which thunder spoke so ominously. We were growing as restless as herded stock.

A man who appeared to have punched open the swinging kitchen doors appeared to stand in for the force of the thunder. Striding into our midst, he towered over the dining tables and chairs. His jet hair was lacquered into a gleaming pompadour. His tuxedoed chest heaved like a trampoline from which his booming voice vaulted over us.

He introduced himself as the owner of *La Bussa*. A fact, he explained, we would otherwise not be privileged to know but that the waiter, Furio, was his uncle to whom he owed this candor. Ordinarily he went about his business incognito.

"The family makes nudo its heart at such momenti. *Purtroppo.*"

It was clear that he appeared onstage reluctantly, but with sure intent. The pectoral thrust of his delivery called attention to what I belatedly recognized as the profile of a concealed weapon bulging over his heart.

"I am here *ecco*. Now you know it. I have zio mio to thank. You are all the cause of this. Welcome. Benvenuti tutti."

Every word was accompanied by the sound of his teeth clacking together, and each sentence seemed to be drawn from his mouth and cut loose with a scissoring of his jaws. He clapped his white-gloved hands together like two grindstones mashing grains into a gritty powder.

Only then did I notice how the tables were set with the familiar sunflower- and cornflower-patterned plates, the vermillion-handled flatware and, only for today, Venetian blown goblets artfully fogged with what was imaginably the artisan's last breath.

The fact that the ceremonial trappings of this *memorial* portended sounds of cutlery and glassware, mastication and salivation, rather than mournful gusts of singing and ear-stopping silences, might have prompted the terseness of the restaurateur's clearly impromptu eulogy.

"The dead are *indigesto*. Of course. You come only for the luncheon. *Buon pranzo*."

"Could a more gruesome meal be imagined?" I said aloud to my table companion. In answer to which, he explained that he'd rushed straight to the restaurant from surgery, oblivious to the blood-smeared napkin at his midriff that the assisting nurse had had no time to remove.

"Well, you look the part of the chef at his chopping block," I couldn't resist commenting, as if I were ever-so-cautiously pouring a clear but volatile liquid from one of the doctor's laboratory beakers into an already bubbling test tube. I was nervous under his scrutiny, as were, I imagined, his surgical team. Perhaps his surgeon's costume was infectious.

As Dr Todorow stood, permitting me to unlace his blood-spattered surgical apron, a black-bearded and unknown-to-us waiter appeared, himself aproned from chest to knees, bearing aloft a heaping dish of glazed artichokes that he lowered between us like manna. How many dishes of these improbably delectable infant thistles, stripped of their outer leaves and bronzed in a pool of sizzling butter, had we shared in our years of regular meetings at *La Bussa*?

But did the doctor and I still share an appetite? Involuntarily, I let the bloody apron fall at his feet where he trampled it in the course of taking his seat. I was as edgy in his presence as Furio's pugilistic nephew encouraged me to be.

Todorow, as though making a point, served himself with his knife. But his listless jabs at the soft and glistening flesh heaped before us were, I now realized, the pretext for something he felt obliged to say. It was not gustatory excitement his mouth wanted now, but voice.

And then I detected tears. Todorow's slit eyes oozed. The flow of emotion, with no less sincerity than the welling of bodily juices in an unsutured wound, was unmistakable. Was this a dutiful spasm of grief, designed to match the mournfulness of the occasion, which the feckless nephew had dishonored by impugning his guests' motives?

Todorow replied to my unspoken query with a breathy heaving of his shoulders that was as surprising in the moment as, I now intuited, had been Siri's antics, played out on the stage of Solfried's burial. For this was, indeed, as Todorow brusquely confessed to me, the gritty scene he presently held in his downcast eyes. Were they dripping self-pityingly, to revivify the rainy pall that had been cast over that funereal day? Solfried's funeral – the vampire laid to an unawakeable rest – had yielded the final proof to Todorow of Siri's unfaithfulness. Only in that contrived instant of spontaneous gymnastics had the doctor fully understood how she had been unfaithful to *him*, the lover, in whose care she had so nimbly placed the more beloved husband's heart under the pretense of tendering her own.

"What has this to do with Furio, or Furio with this?" – I might well have asked. Does not the hunger for strong feeling that is whetted by funerals and weddings permit us to speak of ourselves with unreservedly righteous emotion? And where better than a restaurant to be reminded of such cravings? Perhaps, all in all, Todorow was entitled.

Was this evidence that they were tears of rage rather than mourning that I caught in the gutter of my sidelong glance?

Dr Todorow had, after all, performed the surgery that Siri commissioned. "Impeccably," was his assessment of it, at least from a technical perspective. He claimed to possess his technical prowess as preternaturally as a flexed bicep. He swore that, had the patient been known to him then as Siri's husband, it would in no way have compromised his surgical technique, however heart-stopping the revelation of secret wedlock was to be for Solfried's mourners. The technique – Todorow pronounced the T as emphatically as if he were pronouncing his own name – was, he explained, a practiced indifference to what we naively call "the person". Sentiment was not what the surgeon handled in the viscous broth of the thoracic cavity.

Unbidden, our waiter intruded with another platter of artichokes, though the one before us remained virtually untouched. The oily sheen was off the bulbous green blooms and, no doubt, coagulating at the bottom of the bowl. The waiter merely pushed it aside with the same indifference betrayed by our lack of appetite. He set the new dish beside it, sprinkled it with a polite *prego*, and vanished as vaporously as an indrawn breath.

The breath immediately came back into Todorow's voice. It was the gurgling eruption from a drowned man who revives under one last pounding of the lifeguard's fist upon his unrespiring breast. Did I feel the dull ache of the rescuer in my knuckles?

Todorow's hand had already closed upon mine, as though I were the one to be solaced. But I quickly realized that his intent was to armor himself against the judgment I might render in response to his lament.

My self-consciousness at Todorow's curious embrace – a spider crawling over the back of my hand would have been more intimate – deflected my gaze from the diners dressed, one and all, in black. They were nonetheless more evocative of a wedding party than a gaggle of would-be pallbearers. The sound of corks popping jarred me into noticing that the ordinarily blood-red window hangings were cloaked with black bunting. Each of the guests presented a laden fork or a brimming goblet to a tremulous and expectant gullet. Though loud claps of thunder reminded me that blackness was billowing in the sky above us, its hammer-headed impact chimed with the growing raucousness of the festivities.

Oblivious to our surroundings, the doctor resumed his defense of the impeccable surgical procedure, further unsettling my queasy surveillance of the ever-more-gluttonous meal being made of our Furio. "I do not admit to hardness of the heart when I say the patient is better off without his personhood murking the otherwise brilliant light of the surgery."

I could not help but respond unsympathetically:

"Hardheartedness is something we say. But it is also a condition of the muscle to be massaged. 'Touching' is something else we say of the patient's faith in the surgeon. But even your touch, thanks to the conductivity of polished steel, cannot make any sense of how the heart might behave. You don't divulge this to the patient, am I right? You sweeten the prognosis however grim it may be. You moisten your palm on the forehead smeared with a drooping curl. You primp your smile and promise a return to the robustness of youth. You shake the shaky hand to demonstrate your steady grip on the scalpel.

"Well, we both perform our operations on the heart.

"Solfried was *your* case. The play, I wish to say, is mine. That said, you cannot unconfound Siri's shock at Solfried's death. You wish to plead natural causes. But those are not yours to vouch for. What you do promise is the extension of life at your fingertips. And don't forget, I was present when you declared that those fingers of yours performed the bloody ballet effortlessly, even brilliantly.

"But a clot formed afterward. It lodged and then broke free.

"The gooey insippation of phlegm in the bronchial tube mimics that effect, I think. A cough dislodges the obstruction and permits breathing to resume. Breath as clear as daylight. But when a blockage in the aortic tunnel clears, the lights shut off. And you protest that *you* are in the dark? You plead the infinite mysteries of the body. You excuse yourself to the survivors. I've said that we both perform operations on the heart, but isn't the difference now apparent?

"You have violently objected to my use of murder as a theatrical prop. 'Heartless,' no doubt you wanted to say, chary as you must be of inviting a pun. You make invidious remarks about your own handling of the heart, as though I couldn't touch it no matter how much I might have wished to.

"But as Siri reminds you, your empathy, which in

reality is your hubris, is meant to palpate the patient's love for the doctor, whose powers have their own vampiric charisma. The patient is led to believe that you know *everything* the body can tell. You possess the technical terms, after all – thromboid, endocardial inflammation, myocardium, pericardium, and purkinje fibers. Their utterance is proof that your promise is good.

"And don't the patients finally exhale their relief? With that, they tender you their lives. Words and breath – a fair exchange.

"But not Solfried. That body told you nothing. And when his breath ceased, you swallowed the words with which you would otherwise have gone on praising your work."

I felt a hand on my shoulder. The black-bearded waiter, without waiting for us to acknowledge his presence, ceremonially placed yet another steamy, glistering plate of artichokes between us.

"You-ra special favorite, I was aske-ed. But you do not *mangia*. Still I take-a care of you." When he turned away from us, I noticed that where his silk vest was cinched in the small of his back, the bone handle of a scabbarded knife beetled over the waistband of his trousers.

Todorow encouraged me to take up my fork by flourishing his own. He was as nonchalant as if the tined instrument had been handed to him by an attending nurse. I descended more fastidiously into the wound I was exploring. Another thunderclap ruffled the air.

"The play, you complain, offers no succor for even the most patient audience. The play is strict. The play suffers no empathy for the suffering it so brutally inflicts. One does not feel for them, the characters.

"'Who goes to the theater without the expressed desire to feel for someone, or something?' Your question, not mine.

"I certainly do not denigrate the emotional ambition. But *feel for* is too grandiose a term for what audiences are really capable of, unless we speak of acting, emotional fakery. The members of the audience perform in their seats no less histrionically than the actors onstage. They struggle to feel as sensitive as the suffering players.

"I say that the good play leaves the audience feeling for the feeling.

"I offer only sense without meaning, without false promise, murderous suffering without justice nor solacing vendetta. I deliberately give my audience no impetus for self-congratulatory applause. They may wonder if the fault is theirs that they do not *feel for* it. Well, *feel for* is an imperative for the blind, is it not?

"My play will disappoint only those who are blind to the reality that, in truth, they only ever *feel for* themselves. My play is the bandage laid upon the blind but healing eye, as well as the dispassionate surgical probe that occasioned such a dressing. Neither prop nor costume.

"Then haven't you discerned my optimism winking behind the grim mask? Yet they may one day see!"

Todorow's unblinking stare was so detached from his vigorously masticating jaw, it was as if some cranial mechanical linkage had broken. A teardrop of olive oil, pendant from his lower lip, indicated that perhaps the savor of succulent artichoke had fully captured his attention. I marveled. How could he have taken in any more nourishment than my fastidiously prepared words, the feast that is my understanding of the theater?

A discernible *mmmh* of satisfaction passed Todorow's lips, triggering the most illuminating lightning strike yet of this stormy afternoon. In an instant the dining room was plunged into darkness. The electrical outage ran as fast over our awareness as rainwater would have eddied over our shoes had we stepped out into the street. The darkness held a chill that – I was unable to resist the impulse – made me shudder. It prompted me to reach out a hand to my dining partner, who seemed to have vanished as completely from the realm of touch as from that of sight.

For the moment the silence was palpable, broken only by a staccato shattering of china and glassware that, like the blind man's white-tipped cane, made second-hand reference to the presence of the other diners. Lost to the spatial coordinates of the room, they moved clumsily to orient themselves in the sudden dark. Then, perfect silence, the shadow of perfect stillness.

My ears were yet pricked by a name, floated across the gloom, whispering on the surface of and into my consciousness: "Furio. Furio, are you with us?"

Todorow's joke, such as it was, extruded around what I guessed could only be another pillowy mouthful of artichoke, muffling the punchline, causing him to choke on his own laughter. Luckily, I was his only audience within earshot. I held my tongue between my teeth as gingerly as I would hold a mouse by the tail. I imagined pushing the pillow more forcefully against his struggling breath. More forcefully still, I whispered a squeaky riposte:

"Don't play the player with me. I know your humors are only as sincere as your cravings. You are attempting to lighten the darkness. You expect me to *feel* the consolation of my laughter. Would that show my gratitude to you? I do not applaud, as you know.

"Furio is dead and you are making a silly comedy of it. God alone can afford to be so unsentimental. Every doctor knows how to lift his arms in pitiable helplessness or incontestable victory. There is no difference between the two. Maestros do the same, laboring over the emotional heavings of a symphonic body. All godly pretentions sport the same costume.

"We patient mortals had best let death be death, without worrying about our *feeling for* it. Otherwise, having been so naively impressed into the service of your disingenuous therapeutic troupe, we will forever be looking for ourselves elsewhere than where we are."

The dining room lights came blindingly up on a startling scene: Furio's nephew embroiled in a contest of strength with one of the waiters. His sculpted pompadour was sheened to even greater luster with the perspiration of his efforts. His hands, now stripped of white gloves, knuckles burning, shoved his prostrated antagonist up against a wall faux-frescoed with a panoramic view of the Piazza della Signoria in Florence. The nephew's outsized hands got a firmer grip on the red kerchief worn by all *La Bussa*'s waiters and were strangling this particular waiter. The restored electrical power appeared to be conducted directly through the bodies of the two men, crackling with antagonism. The apparent gratuitousness of the violence rendered it all the more incandescent for the patrons rubbing their eyes against such painful illumination.

"The play, my play. Won't it be just like this?"

How could I forego the opportunity to deliver this line?

She is watching me, the understudy. Officially deposed from her stand-in duties, she is even more determined in her desire to play the parts I am playing now. She has rehearsed them all.

She is alert to the yet *unwritten scene* in which the performer can no longer act the part and the understudy must take her place. As the understudy is irresistibly prone to do, Sigrid pricks up her ears for the patiently awaited knock on the dressing-room door, the rushed turn of the knob by the panicky director, the announcement that she must step into the role, as fit for her as the glass slipper in the fairy tale. Of course, for Sigrid this dream has been shattered by the restored solidity of my ankle bone, steely as a hammerhead in its healed state.

Certainly, the final days of rehearsal have found us at a perilous threshold, inviting the next step. Will it land on solid ground? Sigrid watches my movements with an aptly murderous eye.

Murderess would be the part for her to play if the stage were hers, since all of our scenes bleed with it. Our scenes, assembled like clippings from an out-of-sequence movie reel, proffer to the audience the deed without the motive. As Pan Fleet is notorious for saying, "Violence for its own sake, stripped of the soulful trappings of motive, is the perfect nude. It brooks no idealization of physical existence. It is our fatally lascivious reckoning with a presence not to be dreamt of, because it is so implacably, so violently of the here and now." He is adamant that his dictums are not derivative: "Pan

Fleet is no purveyor of a fecklessly painful theater of cruelty or a medicinal dose of Brechtian pedantry, as the critics will no doubt allege in their reviews."

"This is what it is!" he repeats exasperatedly, pointing to the unvarnished stage floor as though his index finger were an artfully thrown dagger. "This!"

Didn't I confirm the truth of Pan's theory in my brutal stripping away of the understudy's studiousness?

But that was only a lesson for her. My truth is different.

Sigrid's intimate scrutiny of me, viscously adhering to my every physical movement and, I don't doubt, hearing in herself the echo of my every line-reading, cobbles together an ever more self-complicating plot of vengeance. A plot against me, the principal performer. Already painfully aware of the precarious condition of her existence, she is a character resentfully miming the diligent self-effacement that is meant to be her vocation.

And now I see how Pan's undisguised loathing for the mime faithfully follows his theory of the drama. It is not hard to imagine the black-lipped, smiling, white-faced, bereted and perhaps blackly-leotarded figure pushing with blind hands against a glass wall, levering his body upon the blushing toes of his bare feet, winking through the glass to court the audience's compassion, and all the while distracting us from the fact that he is seeing through us with great acuity.

I see Sigrid through that glass. Because I know the glass gives a two-sided view, I see how she might be useful to me even as she believes herself to be acting on her own behalf.

I must confess that I am no acolyte of Pan Fleet's theory of the play. I am motivated.

Furthermore, Sigrid does not represent the true aim of my violence. She will be useful. Merely a prop. You could say that, in the studio of her resentment against me, she is already unwittingly drafting what Pan likes to conjure as the *unwritten scene* of my plot, which – I will not apologize! – is a revenge plot.

I did not know that Dr Todorow would become my protagonist. I did not anticipate the plot until his unfaithful hands, delving in the liquefying dark of my open thighs, excited the thought of their efficient dexterity in the pulsing murk of my beloved husband's chest cavity. I should have trusted to the corporeal unfaithfulness of that plunging hand instead of my all-too-disembodied faith in his reputation as a surgeon. His hands, it was said, were never intimidated by the organs they touched, whatever degree of malignancy they exposed.

Well, reputation, like faith, is a word, a breath.

A penultimate rehearsal was to be announced, and by me.

I had hoped that the darkened theater, where I sat cross-legged in my canvas director's chair on the pouting lip of the stage, would throw me into bright relief for the assembled cast and crew who were practicing stunts, folding ladders, lounging on props, and taking their own visibility for granted. Leaning back into the compliant give of my chair, and casually cradling the back of my head in both hands, the better to convey an impression of careless ease, I was conscious of the black void that lay behind me. The multi-tiered well of darkness, bereft of an audience, was as deep as the pool in which my thoughts were swimming.

Before I could clear my throat, in anticipation of which the small circus troupe scattered across the stage had settled into respectful silence, the empty hall filled abruptly with quarrelsome voices.

Had an unruly audience been admitted by a derelict crew of ushers who had turned up at the wrong hour, on the wrong day, to collect tickets?

This distraction had my audience peering beyond my relaxed pose into the echoing hall.

The quarreling voices were in want of a spotlight because of the curiosity they were arousing. One of the hands, appearing onstage before me, read my thought. Already poised atop a well-angled ladder, he gripped a lever, flicked his wrist and threw a spot into the dark with the accuracy of a native hunter spearing a fish.

As the clashing sentences became more audible – we've always appreciated spectacular acoustics in this house – I recognized their meaning. I turned my head, knowing that there was no turning back to the business of the day, about which I had been poised to speak. The audience onstage before me was upstaged by the players stirring the darkness behind me. The spotlight had caught the quarrelers in its embrace and would not let them go. But the necessity of shielding their eyes against this intrusive antagonist did not, for an instant, give the combatants common cause.

"You promised his life. Never mind the violence of the surgical cut, you said. Costumed as you are in that hypocritically blameless white gown, how can you think yourself any less brutal than the murderers I stalk up there on the stage?"

The accuracy of the stagehand's aim with the spotlight appeared to make Siri's mouth burst into flame. The tall, thin dramaturg, looming over her like a protective shadow, thrust his deflecting palm against the discus of light.

"But, scene after scene of it. You yourself complained of so much pointless violence. I'm talking about the killings that are nothing more than a ghoulish frivolity in your world, not the ardent and meticulous caressing of the corpuscle upon which I swear an oath. If that sounds like pomposity, at least the breast I beat sometimes resuscitates.

"*Trauma*turg you are. Your histrionic language. The knife in your hand. The bloody fingers. How much evidence do you need? Heart renderer! How is the turn of your scalpel edge any less violent and, if it misses its mark, any less frivolous?"

Siri's hand, a sharp-taloned bird, flew at the dramaturg's face. Drawing his hand away from his cheek, Todorow marveled at his bloody fingers. He had seen them before, in another scene. Never before had they appeared to be so unbelievable.

An idling stagehand applauded once from the branch of a park tree that sagged yet was sturdy enough to bear the weight of him and his exuberantly kicking legs. Onstage, the light was bright enough to reveal that the tree trunk was rooted in the dinosaur claw of a sun umbrella. The silence that echoed from the smattering of applause had made the antagonists self-conscious. Todorow, still trying to fend off the unwelcome glare of the spotlight, turned full face into that blindness to bellow, "Enough!"

His cheek, still streaming in the chiaroscuro, appeared tear streaked. His face was a half-mask of tragedy. Siri's face, more stricken with the blinding light, was not the other half. She was smiling toothsomely, as if for the flash of a flattering camera.

Striding aggressively in the direction of the spotlight-wielding technician, Todorow must have got his foot tangled around the base of an aisle seat. He – such a long and heavy frame falls hard and far – disappeared into the aisle. The darkness didn't ripple. He might, I thought, just as well be lost at sea, and the words erupted from my lips in bubbles like the last released breath of a drowning man.

Siri, who had managed to swim effortlessly through the dark house, hoisted herself onto the stage behind me. Seizing hold of the wooden pipe-battens – across which my canvas chair back was embossed with the word *director* – she planted a moist kiss atop my head.

That was how I marked the sea change in her allegiance.

Penultimate rehearsal today. A misnomer really. A pretense. There is nothing ultimate.

That will be for me to prove: the irrelevance of rehearsal for what endlessly happens. Mine will be the act that is not *Scene I, Scene II, Scene III*, etc. for the counters rocking in their seats and scratching the itch that is the next page of their programs.

"The play is long." Pan recapitulated the fact that our months of rehearsal had revealed.

"Will anyone sit still for it? I think they will. Forcibly."

Pan has always championed the fact of force, a formulation which he was fond of turning inside out as the *force of fact* – one being unimaginable without the other. That his theater is meant to be nothing less than a forcing house is a conceit he never tires of reprising.

"The elements of the play are the same for the horticulturalist: light, glass, wood, heat, even soil, even the nostril-flaring trace of ripening shit – all of the props of nature. Though in this case, nature is not to be naturalized. We only believe what grabs our attention, the ineradicably sensible fact of it. Think of the slightly deformed stem of a dwarf cherry tree under glass in November. In three months' time, out of season, out of time, the fruit will be forced from the flower, clutching the pit to its pithy heart. The sunless rays of refracted light, focused through the glass panes, will have done their work. It is blind force that makes the fruit so succulent. Within these darkened walls we must exert the same force."

Overhearing this tediously rehearsed script echoing from the back of the house while I awaited my cue to enter stage left, I realized that I had propped my idling body on Gonzogo's iron rack, one hand thoughtlessly tugging on a leather strap used to bind the victim. When the buzzer rang for my appearance, I navigated a path through the backstage shadows. I stubbed my foot against a massive cabinet containing an entire arsenal of pistols, whips, hatchets, razors, blunderbusses. I knocked my knee against the flank of a claw-footed bathtub. I ducked under a loose branch of papery greenery. I hopped over a bust of Sophocles. Before I reached the slice of light shimmering through the unparted curtain, I nearly tripped over a vagrant cricket bat. I pushed the curtain aside to reveal which of the scenes I had not just passed through was set to flash before my eyes.

***

But there is another scene behind the scenes that might be more illuminating to see.

Up a grassy hill strewn with rocks an old man trudged, negotiating the ground more surefootedly with his blackthorn stick than with his rigid high-topped boots. The long gray locks of hair streaked across his scalp appeared to have been set in place with some kind of cosmetic lacquer. Under the pressing heat of the sun they glistened with perspiration. His stooped shoulders were nonetheless unfettered. Their rise and fall resembled more the ratcheting of a mechanical device, laboriously jacking the man toward the crest of the hill, than a body visibly weakening in its increasingly breathless ascent.

Only in his last steps before reaching the slope's modest summit did the old man's posture show signs of crumpling.

Under a cloudless blue dome, he was suddenly and inexplicably cast under an obsidian shadow. It seemed to radiate with the light it obliterated, no less than a sheet of black glass.

The old man's precarious balance had encountered the rush of a mysterious pusher who had obviously got off to a running start. It was an avatar of brutish, malign intent. This antagonist had no doubt crouched in waiting for the moment of the old man's triumph over the summit. From the vantage point of the one ascending, this nemesis would have been undivinable.

The old man fell over backwards and began to gain momentum. His blackthorn stick remained upright, stuck in the mud. He rolled down the hill like a stone hefted by his attacker, bouncing over the grass-buoyed gullies, knobs and declivities of the incline, no less indifferent to those tumultuous physical forces than the stone itself would have been.

No pain-stricken cries agitated the still air.

Pan Fleet had witnessed a miracle of acrobatics so incongruous with the frail physique his eye had followed up and down the slope that he was inspired to wonder what remarkable capacities might be lurking in his own flesh and blood.

The old man lay face down, apparently lifeless. One arm was flung wide. The other was tucked under his abdomen like a broken wing. Both legs were bent as if in vigorous mid-stride, though they were marching in opposite directions. A disembodied boot stood up defiantly in the long grass beside the incongruously aquiline instep of a naked foot, smooth and white as alabaster. One hip was canted toward the streaming sun. A tear in the denim jeans, in the shape of a cat's eye, revealed a pinkish sheen. Precisely what one would expect to see in the purling crevice of a conch shell. Silkiness where one would have expected raw abrasion.

Struck by such a wanton act of violence, Pan Fleet became a tuning fork of rage. He wanted justice for the stricken man. His eye pointed like a rifle barrel to the crest of the hill, though his target, the malign pusher, had vanished. Pan Fleet's threatening shout hung in the air, flimsy smoke from the muzzle of his outrage. He passed the crosshairs of his vehemence over the ridge line once again. Witness to the crime, how could he not feel the passion of vendetta? The question gave him pause. He wondered at this intimation of indwelling character against which, in principle, he was professionally forsworn.

He stooped to examine the mangled body splayed at his feet. The old man's face, turned to the muddy earth, abruptly turned back with a violent guffaw, as if to ridicule Pan's solicitous approach.

The recumbent form came alive with a twitch of the already provocatively canted hip, where iridescent pinkness bulged through the tear in the denim jeans. In an instant the figure was up on its feet, belying no physical effort at all. The springiness of the body seemed nowhere more concentrated than in the motion of one hand, waving in salutation like a pink handkerchief. Looking as though it were about to sop a wet brow, the hand did something unexpected: it dug with enameled nails into the old man's iron gray scalp, tearing it from a scabrous line of glue to reveal a bountiful fall of blond curls over surprisingly narrow shoulders and – the body having now turned fully in Pan Fleet's direction – a heaving roseate bosom.

The torn denims were quickly dispatched with a wiggle of that ever-more-provocative hip. Along with the bared feet straining to rise on blushing toes, the false nudity of the panties revealed by contrast with the pinker flesh of the thighs, the excited wave of her hand, the shucking off of one sleeve of the woolen black watch shirt, and the ever-more-excited signaling to the top of the hill, put Pan Fleet in a trance.

Uncharacteristically gratified not to know what was happening, he followed the young woman's line of sight. The guiding tips of her fingers were ever so subtly rubbing the soft pastel of the sky where it met the thickly furred green of the hilltop. Her artful touch brought into view a young man, the elusive pusher, whose silhouette was now fully revealed, dominating the skyline.

"Jack! Jack!" The name was carried upon a sudden gust of air to the shimmering crest of the hill. The silhouette waved back.

"Jack, it worked!" Now the young woman stared directly at Pan Fleet. He realized that her hand was making a demonstrative gesture in his direction. She was a magician, conjuring the flapping wings of a dove out of the flourish of a multi-colored silk scarf. Pan Fleet flushed with the embarrassment of the spectator become the spectacle. He was the conjured bird.

The young woman's voice rang out excitedly. "Come down!"

The brute arms of the pusher spread wide from his perch at the top of the hill. He slalomed down the slippery slope with such reckless speed that a catastrophic tumble into the rocky trough at the foot of the hill seemed inevitable. But with grudging disbelief, Pan Fleet saw how the tumbling limbs, apparently hurtling toward disaster, turned at the very last moment into an elegant somersault and the young man landed safely in a patch of clover.

The self-satisfied smile that puffed out the young man's shockingly pink cheeks, round as a baby's, gave voice to his pleasure.

"Jack shall have his Jill. Naught shall go ill."

***

The performance itself did not disturb Pan Fleet so much as the performers' artistic manifesto, about which they boastfully prattled on to their unwitting mentor. *He – he* was their great inspiration! Their speech was tense with the desire to meet the impossibly high standard of their tutelage, as though Pan had personally rehearsed them in their insanely fustian and polemical didacticism.

The play is not for the audience. The audience is what the play makes of them. The play must merely be a surprising event, revealing the essential embarrass-

ment of each of us not knowing anything. To wit: an old man turns out to be a young woman.

The young couple, interrupting each other at every turn in the road they wished Pan to travel with them, expanded upon this theme at a nearby tavern that was famous for attracting poets and playwrights. His undesirable acolytes rumored that Pan Fleet's initials had been discovered, carved into the tavern's scarred walnut bar, from which he was confident he had never raised a glass. The tavern stood just outside one of the vandalized wrought-iron park gates that sagged with the ghostly weight of a rioting teenager and consequently was unable to be closed.

Pan Fleet took the performers' manifesto as little more than the desire to stage an uncharitable shaming of the audience, though they insisted any passing stranger would do, the word *audience* was already too pretentious a pretext. In response, he told them their modus operandi held no real menace. Revealing that a disguise was a disguise did not serve sufficiently to baffle reality. He told them he could render no more severe criticism than that. He did, however, confess that he had been baffled by the old man's transformation at the bottom of the hill, but admonished them that he, as the audience, remained unchanged in his susceptibility to bafflement. Mere play with reality and illusion was just child's play. Thus he chided. He reminded this Jack and Jill that a game could indeed be a play, as the Elizabethans surely knew, but it could not be so cynically gamed.

That the young performers were such enthusiasts gave him no solace. He cringed at the thought that they considered him to be the maestro of their homage, as they now referred to the performance. Worse still, they promised to reprise the performance on hilltops world-wide, recruiting an ever-larger cast of characters, until, in principle, almost no one could say they were not part of the performance.

"Who shall gainsay us?" asked Jill.

"Our show will be as ubiquitous as the nursery rhyme," was Jack's fatuous rejoinder.

"You misunderstand my work entirely!" If Pan Fleet were to extricate himself from this tiresome scene of mistaken identity, this was the only viable line left to him.

So, Pan Fleet had not yet written the inimitable Pan Fleet play. If he had, his young protégés would not be parading themselves so fraudulently in his costume. He took this as a challenge. From now on, he might do things differently. There was, after all, something in the pointlessness these brash and deluded performance artists had shown him. The violence meted out to the old man was merely the occasion of the young woman's dis-guise. That was all it revealed, and revelation was all.

"Well," he silently remonstrated, "violence is never a disguise." He clenched his fist around the trembling stub of a pencil and wrote this sentence on a bar napkin. Then, taking no further notice of the performers, and pocketing the scrawled-upon napkin, he made a hasty exit.

"A momentous note to self," he may have muttered under his breath.

***

If Jack and Jill were Pan Fleet's inspiration for *Killer Killing Killers* – I am thinking this as I read the illuminated title on the freshly set marquee – my own reflections upon the episode would be nothing less than a tumbling after. So, I won't.

"Violence is never a disguise." I enunciated my tutelary repetition of these words to the rehearsing cast members with knife-blade precision.

We had suffered our share of bloodletting accidents during the months of rehearsals. And now, just two days from opening, an actor suddenly stumbled into the midst of our rehearsal to prove the point.

Amid his fellows awaiting their cues backstage, he had feigned opening the veins at his wrist as a witty show of boredom. It was a prop knife, toothed nonetheless for appearance's sake. He was sure he had turned the serrations of the blade away from his flesh, but here he was, staggering uncomprehendingly through the curtains and into the wash of the key lights illuminating the actors, those who were actually meant to appear in the scene we were rehearsing. The actor was aghast at the spectacle of so much blood spurting vehemently from his body.

"A most eloquent gash." I muffled the utterance with a heavy breath.

"Call an ambulance!" I cried aloud.

It must be said that this unheralded actor, urgently in need of a tourniquet, made his appearance immediately after my utterance of the word "violence". His uncued entrance, bloody and belated as it was, must have precluded his hearing it.

Yet he was exemplary.

***

Let me not wax too didactic, pompous though that may

sound. It is enough to say I was a child once. I know the pangs of uncontrollable emotion.

At the age of five I was already an intrepid theater-goer. My shiny navy-blue suit, my matching bow tie clipped to the collar of my crisp white shirt, my black patent leather shoes sparkling like jewels when I lifted them from their box in the back of my closet, my hair combed and lacquered with the scent of lavender, my hand held out for my mother's as the taxi honked its horn. All this was the make-up for my performance of "sensitive child". As we were guided to our seats, the usher took my mother's arm with apparently the same degree of affection that she held on to mine. We sat in dying light. Our pulses quickened. My mother encouraged me to breathe deep, draw the darkness into me and hold it there. She promised me that when I exhaled, a world would come to light, as though the kiss of life trembled upon my lips.

My mother wept uncontrollably at our first attendance. I still remember the line that pinched her eyes closed: "What's Hecuba to him, or he to Hecuba ...?"

I marveled at how the moist tongue of the actor's delivery had licked the corners of my mother's eyes, to form droplets that she stowed covetously in the folds of her handkerchief, embroidered at its edges with throbbing pink hearts. The liquid emotion of the actor's delivery did nothing to aid my comprehension of what heaved in her breast at that moment.

The actor's line was not sad, unless sad was a word my young mind did not fully understand. But I knew tearfulness. Perhaps it was the theater itself that inspired the actor's grief. Hunched under a dimly lit dome swimming with ominous shadows, the audience-laden tiers of seats seemed certain to collapse upon one another like the folds of a breathless accordion. The stage itself was muffled with a surround of musty drapery. The sound of coughing was scattered throughout the trapped air of the hall; intimations of slow suffocation.

So, in my high-pile velvet seat, while inhaling air that seemed to have already been breathed by countless ghostly others, I was reminded of nothing more than the funeral home where I slumped, in a seat as plush and as overshadowed with gloom as this one, beside my father's open coffin. Then, too, I heard weeping all around me, as steady as the fall of rain on slate shingles. The guttering aura of a single candle rustled the shadows of the adult mourners who were seated round the coffin, and I saw, as in a theater, how, at what could only have been my mother's command, the man in the coffin wore a disguise.

My father's face, during my entire time on this earth, had been artfully bearded. The heavy black moustache was the handle that went with his spade-shaped goatee. He had worn gold-rimmed spectacles. They held his sparkling eyes as a jewel box holds diamonds. His long, thick hair combed straight back, reached from his forehead almost to the nape of his neck.

But the man in the coffin was clean shaven. His cheeks, however sallow, glistened no less than the dripping wax of the candle. His hair was shorn to the length of a much younger man's, one ambitious to present himself to the world as well groomed, a desirable prospect. My dead father now wore the mask of his youth. From awkwardly posed and poorly focused photographs, I knew this was exactly how he'd looked on the day he proposed marriage to my mother.

Though the tears I shed were indistinguishable from the baubles decorating the cheeks of the other mourners, they pricked my face with salty rage. I might have asked the same question that was to stir my mother's deep feeling one year later: "What's Hecuba to him?" If, that is, Hecuba were my father's name and I were *him*. The answer would have come without the tears, since the question, in that case, would have been answerable in a word: nothing.

***

Years later, by then a serious student of theater, as much as my mother's well-groomed *aficionado*, I attended the performance I'd always hoped I was training for, the performance that would inspire an inner feeling, fully commensurate with the actor's word and gesture, as my mother had felt it. Indeed, the strength of her feeling had caused me to doubt my own capacity for it.

That it was a new play by a rather aged little-known playwright, who had lain fallow for at least a decade, boded well, I thought.

When I took my rigid and uncushioned hardwood seat in the first balcony row of the newly constructed auditorium, *The Unexpected Theater*, I understood at once what the visionary architect had intended. By raking the seats on bare steel scaffolding, so that the aisles and the catwalks between the rows of seats were suspended in empty space, the audience would possess as penetrating a view of the basement beneath their dangling feet – with its bustle of technicians amidst a vast labyrinth of props and mechanical devices for maneuvering them – as of the space above their heads. Not to mention the stage itself.

Uncurtained, and as sweeping as the panoramic view in nature one has to turn one's head from side to side to appreciate, the stage was also as deep as a landscape painting rendered in exhaustive perspective. One could see straight through the fantasias of dramatic staging to the massive steel-clad wall at the back of the stage.

On that stage, where nothing could be hidden from the audience's view, in which all of the devices of theatrical illusion were undisguised, I found myself unexpectedly to be a sensitive of the theater.

So it began.

Once enveloped in darkness, the audience was given a keyhole view of an iron bed. A lens mounted on the light source would have shown light carving the darkness. The blanketed forms of a man and a woman appeared inert, sleeping. Their peaceful somnolence was then violently shaken by loud thunderclaps emanating from recessed speakers mounted on the side walls of the theater. I had, before the house lights came down, noticed how the speakers resembled nothing so much as the flesh-covered cartilage of human ears.

Awakened by the thunderclaps, the husband was up, circling the bed in which his wife was revealed in pregnant nudity by the downturned covers from which he had leapt. She was writhing back and forth as though gripped in the full-blown torment of a nightmare.

Holding her belly with both hands, she might have been struggling to preserve its porcelain sheen against the shattering force of what I took to be uterine contractions. The infant's limbs appeared to be storming within her as violently as the speakers conveyed the weather, now strobed with lightning throughout the auditorium. Downstage, a wind machine whined in the dark. Everyone in the audience must have felt the intimacy of that breath on their faces.

Perhaps it was some part of the wife's now audible pleading with her husband.

The husband, still circling the bed, hands over his ears, torqueing his head back and forth, cried out over his wife's wails. But he could not stifle her demands. She might have been calling to him from within the womb itself, where, she exclaimed, the unborn child was lost in a storm-battered forest. She wanted to know why the father could not hear the child's voice crying for its father.

The husband circled round and round the bed in an ambit that appeared to deny him a means of escape from his wife's nightmare.

The thunder and lightning stormed unrelentingly above them.

When the wife cried out again from the dream womb, she beseeched her poor husband to find her. She cried out that she was lost in the stormy forest, forsaken, with the child hanging perilously at her breast. She shrieked at the trees looming over her. Still prostrated on the bed, she nonetheless appeared to be navigating a sinuous path, as though trying to find her way back to her husband. Her feet padded the air. With wild gesticulations, she recoiled from the scabrous branches. She tore ropey vines away from her face. Her voice sounded as if it were being shredded in the branches of wind-bent trunks, deep in this forest from which no human footsteps ever led. Unless...

Unless the husband, in his hectic circling of the bed on bare human feet, might happen upon it, as in a dream. Yes, in a dream – how could it be otherwise?

The question suddenly thumped in my chest, and others swiftly followed. Which was the womb? Which the world? Which was the reality? Which the dream? Which was the reeling mind, and which the circling body?

There, there was the drama itself! It was kicking in those tumultuous questions no less than the baby kicking in the wife's dreaming body.

My eyes were wet. I could feel sweat trickling between my shoulder blades. My hands clung to the first-row balcony rail as tightly as someone fearful of being carried off in a hurricane. There was no coming in from the storm. It was the same weather inside and out.

Was this heart-pounding breathlessness in the cavity of my chest not the empathy that my mother's tears had so eloquently exemplified for me on our many pilgrimages to the theater? I beheld her tears then as if at a great distance. I squinted through them now. Clutched – as I felt I was at this moment – in an intimate embrace with the actors onstage, I did not wish to wriggle free from the impending dénouement.

But there was to be no finale.

The actors, enveloped in the wife's dream but becoming ever more palpably real to the audience, were surely serving the hand of a brilliant and inspired theater director. For in the concluding moments of the performance – the husband circling the bed, the wife rocking her belly from side to side in the bed – the actors had obviously been instructed to gradually slow their physical movements until they achieved a kind of underwater balleticism, impeccably calibrated. The gifted director surely meant to evoke the choreography that we all once performed in the viscous medium of the amniotic sac. As the storm abated, the physical movements of the actors slowed to a stop. Beginning or end? We were not told. The lights came up.

Our smugly ironic psychiatric practitioners tell us that the frictionless physical ecstasy that we dream of incessantly, and that is awakened in the sexual act, is a memory of the womb. No doubt the critics would say that the meaning of this play could be midwifed only by this memory.

But the performance was such that I was not thinking of what I could more viscerally feel, as some residual stickiness, once the waters had broken in the palms of my exuberantly clapping hands.

Thus did I at long last *feel* for them, the actors.

***

On returning home from my epiphany at *The Unexpected Theater*, I relished giving the rendition of the play that my mother would demand, tucked up as she was those days in taut satin covers, swaddled in her sickbed. The massive four-poster – carved of black walnut at the head and foot boards, in which myriad antique figures, naked except for their armor and weaponry, were featured in combat – could have given wide berth to three grown men, whereas the frail form of the woman who had given me birth barely made a dent in the mattress. At my insistence, the bed had been positioned to face the grand proscenium of the picture window, giving her a view of the uppermost floors of the facing skyscrapers. She might then imagine they were props hung on flimsy wires from an invisible grid, the existence of which was made persuasive by the well-appointed light that shone forth from it. To be perfectly frank, there wasn't much to see. But once the curtains were parted, in the early morning, perhaps there was much to expect.

So how could it happen that I, still so vividly possessed of strong feeling for the actors' passionate performance, and thus so well-prepared to make my mother weep for them, was destined, upon my appearance at her bedside, to find my mother dead in her sleep? For a briefly held breath I imagined that the resemblance to sleep was the reality.

Indeed, I wept.

***

I had ardently wished that my new-found capacity for empathy might provide a more convincing bond with my mother, who was, as things turned out, only herself, as I was myself. And that was proof of my self-deception. There is no *act* of pathos unless you count the artful self-discipline of the actor, which can therefore never be the path to another real person. Worse yet, it is only a path to the pose of another person. No. Empathy is only for oneself. Sitting rigidly by my mother's bedside, I had never been more aware of being myself, by myself, without pathos, unexpectant of empathy, as each of us ought to reconcile ourselves to be, knowing, as we must, how irreconcilably apart we are from each other and always will be. This fact we know no more passionately than when in the presence of the dead.

***

Jack and Jill went up a hill ... One came tumbling after.

Since childhood, I have been haunted by the indifference of the rhymer to the violence in that poem. A child's rhymer at that. But I have learned that if feeling cannot be felt for another, it is in that way no more than a pail of water. If empathy is an obstacle to this feeling because, for all the children who are now grown up, empathy is after all only an *act*, the would-be feeler, feeling hopelessly for his feeling self, will only find himself clenching his resentful fist ever tighter. Perhaps the banishment of feelings altogether is our only hope. Perhaps then we can start again, from feeling.

This is why my métier in the theater is violence. Violence is not solaced by feeling. It is feeling without the trappings, without the traps.

Which is precisely why I say that the actor – who, as I

have already mentioned, stumbled through the curtains on the day of our penultimate rehearsal, bloodied by an unintended act apparently more gruesome than the written scene we were rehearsing – that actor was exemplary.

Yes, exemplary. There he was, interrupting the rehearsal scene with a disbelieving look on his face, feeling the blood sluice through his fingers, and convinced in his bloody fingers that disbelief is not a suitable alternative to a tourniquet. And we who dutifully called the ambulance, compassionately ministered to his wound with rags and advised him to raise his hand above his head, succumbed to the feeling that we might be witnessing a loss of life, a life that nonetheless persisted without drama since the wound turned out to be superficial.

October 17

There was never to be an ultimate or final rehearsal. Pan Fleet did not indulge such self-dramatizing ceremonies. The success of the rehearsal is unrehearsed.

"Play on." Pan Fleet's parting words to us before opening night were intended to be the kind of indefinite imperative which the uninitiated ingénue, shoved violently into the spotlight without a script, would be obliged to understand simply as the next thing that happens. The thing that happens next is undeniably a kind of violence, after all. Not to mention the hazing of the understudy.

The next thing that happened, a few frantic hours before the opening night curtain-raising, was a suspiciously melodramatic phone call I received. It announced the abduction of our star performer by bacterial agents. A violent cough had seized her by the throat, Siri explained. Her voice was gone. "The understudy must serve," she croaked with her last vocable breath. The connection went dead.

Nor was the dramaturg available for consultation. I imagined his finger on some fainting pulse, flickering in the wards, begging for his imminent appearance in surgery. The simple fact was, he no longer belonged in the midst of action that must now happen without a dramaturg's useless commentary.

Sigrid, the understudy, brilliantly performed the part for which she was the substitute actor. Perhaps her knowledge of herself as a substitute was the secret of her success. Acting, for an actor, could not be a more authentic act. It is singular and it is plural, like every passing moment of our days. And what did our play attempt to do, after all, but pass for such experience without passing it by? *Killer Killing Killers*. Even my least charitable critics would have to applaud the challenge to the actor, to be all of the killers killing and yet each individually. But would they appreciate the killing itself, the essential violence? It is the life of death. This is the essence of what I mean by my title. Singular, plural.

From Icon's first pistol shot, I might have been a runner in the race of scenes. I watched the performance feverishly from my wooden sentry box that had been wheeled, at my instruction, into a blind spot just off-stage right. It was a kind of hunter's blind, I suppose, with a laddered perch high enough to take in the entire stage floor. Narrow as a confessional, it stood like an upended coffin, and was fitted with a window, much like a ticket booth. With such a viewfinder, I would be well positioned to inventory what I had imagined with such steely severity, the (dare I say) musical variations on the violence of killing, by the killer, Sigrid, killing and killing. Singular, plural. It happens just so. Who, in all good conscience, can say otherwise?

The scenes moved, slick as celluloid, across the glass screen of my viewfinder, as if I were both the camera-man and the projectionist in one fell stroke of creation. In order not to miss a single detail, I also followed the montage on the moistened tip of my index finger, turn-ing the pages of the script from each corner, one by one, scene after scene.

Allowing for costume changes, Sigrid played them all as though she were cast adrift in the flow of a raging tor-rent. There was Smartson stooping over his wife's hacked carcass, Mangan smartly tilting a ladle of molten lead into Kenton's sizzling gullet, Balustrade wringing Lawrence's neck, Agave plunging the sword into Cli-max's already pinned torso, Rosalinda thrusting the nee-dle between Gonzogo's lips and spitting blood from her tongue, Ho wielding a blade in place of the missing cricket bat, sending Hum's head flying into the first row of the stalls, Hamlet shooting into the bleeding wall of the seaside hotel room, Marvin impaling Klaus's hand with a serrated steak knife. Marvin again ripping off the wig, wiping the knife blade on a pleat of his skirt before rushing from the restaurant cloakroom, and Midge silently dropping the swaddled infant down the laundry chute. Then the filthy, porcelain-tiled subway station. A line of commuters brimming at the platform's edge. As the tall blond man with the short green oxygen tank slung over one shoulder steps forward, his arms thrust out for the homicidal push, I suddenly wondered ...

Who is this marauding onto my stage?

UNENDING (October 18)

The detective strode briskly ahead of me, quite oblivious to the fact that I had already plotted his footsteps for him. His every move from this point on had been blocked for my staging. Though he had hoarsely commanded that the stage lights be brought up, his girth and the heavy swing of his trench coat curtained my view. Scurrying in his wake, I missed the moment when he seized Sigrid by the shoulders, knocked the green oxygen tank to the floor, and arrested her mid-murder, the murder she was meant to commit in the final scene of *Killer Killing Killers*. This was, of course, not the crime for which she would be taken into custody. Though I missed the fateful moment of her capture, there was no denying that it had transpired.

Several uniformed officers, entering from the rear of the stage, were already laying hands on the actors who were queueing for the train that now would never arrive.

This raid – if that's what it will be called when written up for official scrutiny – must be viewed through my eyes first, under my direction, not Pan's.

The telephone report of Dr Todorow's murder was my curtain-raiser. I had dialed at precisely the moment when, I imagined, Icon would be pointing his pistol: Scene 1. Synchronicity seemed important. I wished to act at the identical moment, just before it passed on into the next.

The crime scene was, however, mine alone, blocked and dressed for a more original effect. The blue velvet curtains in Dr Todorow's apartment were drawn across the panoramic window, blocking what would otherwise have been a splendid view into his penthouse from the building opposite, where his goggle-eyed neighbors yearned to see what he was doing or what was being done to him. The door to his bedroom was flung open so that the brilliant lighting within would shine accusatorily upon the pooled blood at the bedside. This would have the added effect of lengthening the shadows of the living room furniture, as if they – divan, side tables, magazine rack, floor lamps, and an architect's drawing-table – were all in motion, in flight from whatever violence had been unleashed in the adjoining chamber.

But that was just staging. There was action to be reckoned with too, so that even the most circumspect investigative eye would detect a compelling, even a coercive narrative. Here I was obliged to think like an understudy.

What would the murderous wife have most ready to hand as a weapon? And since the weapon would have been premeditatively made ready to hand, where must it lie? A hammer under the pillow. The head returns nightly, reliable as a recurring dream. The hammer is as hard as the head against the pillow, but harder.

And so, the claw of the hammer, having bitten into the back of the victim's head, would explain the blood trail into the living room, where Todorow's body could drag itself no further than the border of an oriental carpet. The furniture in the room had rested its feet upon that carpet for years. The deep imprints in the pile would permit a diligent detective to reconstruct the arrangement of the furnishings, in case they had been moved. But I had left everything in place. Finally, the crimson dye in the weave of the oriental carpet was a perfect match for the wine color of death.

After having made my telephone report, I placed the phone in the victim's hand, as though he had hoped to save himself by calling for help. My husband had likewise hoped that the doctor might save him, and by the very same hand. Now I had made it abundantly clear that all such hope is theatrical flummery.

So when the detective, whom I had unofficially followed to the theater, finally took Sigrid in hand, I was confident that the oxygen tank at her feet would be of no further use to her.

Though the other actors caught up in this *unwritten scene* began to protest this interruption of the performance, calling to one another for help and jostling the invading uniforms that were not mere costumes, a low roar began to fill the station that could easily have been mistaken for the arrival of a train.

The boisterous detective broke off the droning litany of his commands. Out of what appeared to be almost childish curiosity, he padded gingerly to the edge of the subway platform, listening for the train. Dipping his head deep into the murk of the auditorium, and swiveling his gaze back and forth, he cautiously observed, "But ... there's no audience. There's no audience here at all."

The remark was directed to me where I stood, inches away. Over his shoulder I could make out the figure of Sigrid being led towards an exit by an officer so decorous, with his hand placed lightly upon her waist, he might have been leading her into a waltz.

I answered mysteriously: "It's dark. So you never know."

Also available from grand**IOTA**

APROPOS JIMMY INKLING
Brian Marley
978-1-874400-73-8   318pp

WILD METRICS
Ken Edwards
978-1-874400-74-5   244pp

BRONTE WILDE
Fanny Howe
978-1-874400-75-2   158pp

THE GREY AREA
Ken Edwards
978-1-874400-76-9   328pp

THE SHENANIGANS
Brian Marley
978-1-874400-78-3   220pp

Alan Singer is the author of five previous novels, most recently *The Inquisitor's Tongue*. He also writes about aesthetics and the visual arts. He is professor of English and a member of the MFA faculty in fiction at Temple University.

Cover image: Edward Hopper, *The Sheridan Theater* (see acknowledgments page for credits)

Production of this book has been made possible with the help of the following individuals and organisations who subscribed in advance:

Neil Atkinson
Peter Bamfield
Chris Beckett
Lillian Blakey
Andrew Brewerton
Ian Brinton
Jasper Brinton
Peter Brown
Robert Caserio
John Cayley
Claire Crowther
Elaine Edwards
Allen Fisher/Spanner
Jim Goar
Giles Goodland
Fred Grand
Penny Grossi
John Hall
Andrew Hamilton
Randolph Healy/Wild Honey Press
Peter Hughes

Kristoffer Jacobson
Graeme Jukes
Richard Makin
Michael Mann
Alan Marley
Askold Melnyczuk
David Miller
John Olson
Merle Olson
Sean Pemberton
Lou Rowan
James Russell
Maurice Scully
Pablo Seoane Rodríguez
Valerie Soar
Lloyd Swanton
Eileen Tabios
Visual Associations
Keith Washington
Alastair Wilson
Anonymous x 2

www.grandiota.co.uk

ing Source UK Ltd.
Keynes UK
V010634270920
2UK00001B/24